Ethan

Delaney Diamond

Garden Avenue Press

Chapter One

Bluetooth in his ear, Ethan Connor paced his office atop the building he owned in the middle of Atlanta.

"Why did I hire you?" he demanded of the asset manager on the line. He stopped moving and listened to the response before interrupting. "Those are excuses. We don't cut corners. If there's a structural problem, call the engineer and get a proposal to fix the issue. Then send me the new budget. I want both on my desk first thing tomorrow morning."

With an angry movement, he removed the Bluetooth and stalked over to his desk, an enormous U-shaped structure made of black American oak with silver painted wood feet. On top were two laptops, one of which he opened to start the workday as he always did—by sorting emails.

He sent a note to his in-house broker for a status update on a property under contract. Then he read a memo from an asset manager in Denver who informed him that capital improvements on a newly acquired office building had been completed early, and financial projections were on track for the next quarter.

While reviewing an expense report, a soft knock on the double doors interrupted his concentration. "Come in," he called.

His executive assistant, Daria, entered carrying a leather-bound notepad tucked against her side and approached his desk. Middle-aged with toffee-colored skin and a rounded figure, Daria had worked for him the better part of eight years. A dependable member of his team who knew when to speak, when to be quiet, and could be trusted with the most sensitive information.

"I didn't see you come in, yet here you are. Please tell me you didn't spend the night in your office," she said.

"Okay, I won't tell you."

He spent a lot of time at work, putting in long hours every week, and the past couple of days had been no different. Everyone in his life thought he worked too hard. The women, anyway. His girlfriend Skye, his mother, who constantly dropped not-so-subtle hints about wanting more grandchildren, his sisters, his personal assistant, Layla, and Daria.

His office design fit his rigorous schedule. It was the size of an apartment and included a full bathroom. A private dining room accommodated late night meals alone or when meetings with business associates ran late. A conference room behind glass afforded soundproof privacy, and there was an open area with a burgundy leather chair and two black leather couches on opposite sides of a glass coffee table, one of which adjusted into a full-size bed. The only other color in the black and white office was a plush burgundy guest chair in front of his desk. Even the photos on the wall of the buildings he owned were printed in black and white.

There were lots of windows, but the half-drawn shades behind him currently obscured the view and blocked the morning sun.

Daria let out a dramatic sigh but didn't comment further, knowing it was a waste of her time.

"They emailed the contracts from London—nine o'clock last night," she said, eyes bright behind the black-framed glasses perched on her nose.

"Someone worked late over there," Ethan remarked.

"Very late, considering the six-hour difference."

"Guess they didn't want to lose the deal after all," he said dryly.

The London deal had been a thorn in his side, forcing him to fly to the UK months ago because of problems with permits and other issues he had not been made aware of in a timely manner. He had spent way too much energy trying to fix the problem and arguing back and forth over other issues, only to be told the renovations still might not go through.

He finally realized his English "partners" were trying to squeeze more money out of him, but he also recognized he had the upper hand. A position he loved to be in. True enough, he would suffer losses if he walked away, but they were destined to suffer even more. He played hardball and threatened to cancel the project if they couldn't meet his demands.

Lucky for him, they didn't call his bluff and scrambled to save the contract before the eight o'clock deadline this morning.

"I should make them wait on my signature," Ethan said.

Daria laughed, knowing full well he was going to sign. He might be able to bluff them, but he couldn't bluff her.

"I forwarded the message before I came in," she said.

Ethan opened his email and reviewed the contract, with Daria referring to her notes regarding specific items he'd requested. After they made sure the required clauses were included and the ones he didn't want were excluded, he electronically signed and submitted the contracts.

Daria headed for the open door. "Have you decided what

you plan to do for lunch today?" She looked over her shoulder, hand on the door knob.

"Make a reservation for me at Notte."

"A celebratory lunch?" she asked.

"Absolutely. I've earned it and so have you. Buy yourself lunch on me."

"I already made reservations. You were kind enough to send me flowers too. They'll arrive before I leave work this evening." Daria smiled and closed the door.

Chuckling to himself, Ethan shook his head and strolled over to the drafting table where the plans for his biggest project to date were laid out.

He'd worked his whole life for a project like this and couldn't be prouder. Mixed-use communities were nothing new in Atlanta, but Horizon was the first one southeast of the city.

In conjunction with investor-partners, Connor International Industries had almost completed phase one of the five billion-dollar development, which included space for retail stores and restaurants, one thousand rental apartments priced from mid-range to luxury, and a public park. After the last two phases were completed, the final product would consist of more retail space, single-family homes, a few hotels, and office space.

In addition to the usual walkability and convenience of the work-play community design, he'd brought on an environmental consultant. Among other recommendations, they suggested building geothermal homes and a community garden. Instead of one, Ethan added two gardens, one of which the restaurants already used to provide farm-to-table ingredients in their dishes.

If all went well, in a few years Horizon would be a complete and fully occupied, smoothly functioning community. His greatest accomplishment. Yet...

He frowned. Each year, he achieved greater and greater success. Each year, he worked harder and made more money, but lately he was beginning to wonder what else he could do. There was some goal, some achievement he was missing, but he'd figure it out soon enough.

Until then, he'd bask in the glory of his grandest project.

Ethan stepped out of his office shower and plucked the large, fluffy blue towel from the towel warmer. He and his personal trainer worked hard on weights this afternoon and included a run around the indoor track. He felt energized and ready for the evening's event—his youngest brother's graduation party. It was supposed to be a small affair with only a handful of guests, but knowing his stepfather's penchant for a party, there would likely be dozens of people at the house.

After drying off and splashing on cologne, he changed into a dark blue suit with a cranberry and cream horizontally striped tie. He double-checked his appearance in the oval mirror and smoothed a hand over the day old stubble lining his jaw. He'd have to shave later at home. Skye didn't like facial hair.

He sent a text to his personal assistant, instructing her to purchase a shaving kit he could keep at the office.

Then he left, taking the elevator to the first floor where his chauffeur, Halston, waited with the limo door open.

"Mr. Connor," the big man said. He wore a black uniform and cap, and as a former Navy Seal had the build and square jaw to match.

"Halston." Ethan climbed into the back and settled in for the ride to pick up Skye at one of his many properties, The Rose Hotel, which he'd named after his mother. He kept a deluxe suite there for when he didn't want to drive to his mansion outside the city.

They pulled up in front of the hotel, and before Halston could leave the driver's seat to open the door, Ethan's foot hit the pavement in anticipation of seeing Skye. He received unprecedented pleasure from watching her simply walk toward him.

She exited the doors, and he drew in a deep breath. After a rough couple of days, seeing her loosened the tightness inside him. The frustrations of the day faded and he immediately relaxed.

Skye Thorpe was a tawny-skinned goddess in an eye-catching cape dress in cranberry-red with gold heels. The red matched the red in his tie, thanks to the diligence of his personal assistant.

Her thick, lustrous hair was swept up on top of her head, and gold hoops adorned her ears. She had the type of body traditional media frowned upon, but he found irresistible as she came toward him with the sexiest damn walk he'd ever seen on a woman. His eyes ate up every curve of her voluptuous body—a body with breasts, ass, and hips galore. She strode toward him like the entrance was a runway, and he tossed around the idea of skipping the party and taking her to bed since they hadn't seen each other for several nights. He longed to plant his hands on her wide hips and take his time sucking on her luscious breasts.

She'd put a spell on him. There was no other way to explain how, after seven years, she continued to capture his attention simply by making an appearance, much like she did the very first time he'd seen her in the hotel bar. She'd been upset and disappointed because some loser stood her up, and he'd become the luckiest man on the planet when he rescued her from a disappointing night.

Skye sidled up to him—a smile on plump red lips as inviting as a siren's song—filling the air around them with the scent of her perfume. He slipped an arm around her back and drew her close, gazing down into her dark brown, upturned eyes.

She laughed, knowing he intended to kiss her, because he always did whenever they spent time apart. He had to kiss her. He had to touch her. He had to experience the full power of Skye.

"You're going to mess up my lipstick."

"Reapply it."

He fastened his mouth over hers, kissing her with passion and the assurance of knowing this woman belonged only to him. He let a hand slide lower in a possessive grab of her bottom. Halston remained silent beside the car, eyes respectfully averted.

Skye moaned, and that little sound sent an electric charge straight to Ethan's groin.

When he lifted his head, he still didn't let her go. He pressed his hard length into her soft belly. "I hate I have to wait to get you home. It's been too long."

"It's been two days," she pointed out, a smile of pleasure brightening her face.

"An eternity," he said.

"And whose fault is that? You're the one who decided to stay at the office last night when you could've been here, in bed with me."

"Too distracting, but maybe that means my priorities are all screwed up."

"Yes, they are, but I forgive you."

She swiped her thumb across his lips, removing the lipstick transferred from her mouth. "And please, shave all of *that* off as soon as possible." She slipped into the car.

"Yes, ma'am," Ethan said with amusement, following her.

Halston closed the door behind them, and they were on their way.

Chapter Two

As Skye exited the limo, she nodded her thanks at Halston as he helped her from the car. She held a red gift-wrapped box in her hand. Tonight, the Connor-Santanas were celebrating Maxwell Santana's graduation from medical school and the subsequent starting of his residency in a few months. The whole family was proud, and she and Ethan were joining them at his mother's home for the celebratory party.

Speaking of Ethan...

Skye turned halfway up the stairs. Ethan came slowly toward her, phone attached to his ear.

She cast a disapproving frown at him. "Baby, you can't go in there with the phone to your ear," she chided in a whisper.

At times it seemed his work was never done. Despite his amorous greeting, he'd ignored her the entire ride as he talked in low tones to one of his employees in the Hawaii office. She only heard snippets of the conversation, but there seemed to be a problem with the condominiums in Oahu.

He either didn't hear her chastisement or was ignoring it

and kept walking, stopping one stair above her. He turned, a vision of power in a pair of Ferragamo Gancini Oxfords and broad shoulders wrapped in a bespoke navy-blue suit, blocking the light.

Powerful men were an aphrodisiac. Handsome men were too. Ethan was both. He had great bone structure in a classic male face and skin a dark shade of mahogany.

"The phone," Skye said.

She raised an eyebrow to convey she was serious, and he needed to wrap up the conversation. His eyes narrowed. He didn't like being told what to do, but she held her ground.

"When do you think you'll hear from them?" he asked the person on the line.

Skye rested one hand on her hip, so he knew she meant business. Face tightening with resignation, Ethan took several steps away and continued talking, and Skye waited impatiently for him to end the call.

While she waited, a silver Bentley pulled up, and she smiled politely at the new arrivals. She didn't recognize them and assumed they must be friends of the family because she knew all of Ethan's stateside family on his mother and stepfather's side.

With the conversation ended, Ethan approached Skye and extended his arm. "Happy now?" he asked.

She squeezed his firm biceps and experienced a brief thrill, her nipples tightening a little. Ethan took good care of his body, and she was a lucky woman indeed to have all that hard muscle to herself.

She leaned against his powerful frame, taking delight in the combination of his unique male scent and his cologne. He always smelled crisp and clean—like peppermint, but not peppermint.

"Very happy. You know good and well your mother

wouldn't tolerate you coming into her house while you were still working, and I'd be the one in trouble for letting you do it."

He let out a low laugh—very masculine, very smooth, very Ethan—which softened his profile in such an achingly handsome way, her chest hurt. He could be so serious at times, because of work and the responsibilities of running a multibillion-dollar real estate empire, that she appreciated the moments when he relaxed and enjoyed himself.

Anyway, she knew why he'd been amused by her comment. No one *let* Ethan do anything. He did as he pleased, and though she'd been stern about him putting away the cell phone, she was well aware he did so because he wanted to, not because she made him.

At the top of the stairs, he let her walk ahead of him, his warm hand touching the base of her spine. Two male attendants swung the doors open, as if presenting royalty to their subjects, and she and Ethan glided through.

The foyer of the mansion was an opulent showpiece. A table with decorative items sat in front of three arches that led to the rest of the first level, and a sweeping, bifurcated staircase with wrought-iron balustrades led to the second floor. Geometric images were carved into the white epoxy concrete floors, which shone under antique chandeliers hanging from the two-story ceiling.

They made their way through the middle arch and into the high-ceilinged great room where most of the guests had gathered. Waitstaff dressed in all black circulated among the invitees with small trays of drinks. Other members of the staff replenished delicious-looking finger foods on tables around the room.

The tastefully designed room temporarily clashed with the blue and gold balloons reaching eight feet high in each corner and a *Congratulations Graduate* banner hanging over the fireplace.

Right away, family and friends approached, and the customary hugs and squeals of pleasure began. As Skye was accustomed to attending family events, she enthusiastically returned the hugs and kisses she received.

Eventually, she and Ethan separated, mostly because various family members wanted to ask Ethan about a business venture they were considering or simply to catch up because he was so busy they hadn't seen him at the last function. She was used to that and went to place the gift they'd brought with the pile of other beautifully wrapped boxes near the fireplace.

Her eyes scanned the room for Maxwell, but she didn't see him. She did, however, catch sight of Ethan's sister Monica as she entered the room.

Monica was her favorite of his siblings. Tall, with a model-like frame, she had an outgoing personality and always spoke her mind, which sometimes did not go over well with the family. Monica was a free spirit. Her social media following of over three million people lived for her antics and straight talk. Recently, she'd cut off all her hair and now sported a near-bald head. The video where she'd shaved her head was her most popular post to date. She wrote one simple word as the caption: Freedom.

Skye started across the room to greet Monica, but Ethan's Aunt Florence blocked her path.

"Don't you look lovely," the older woman beamed. She was his mother's older sister.

Skye bent down and squeezed her plump shoulders before pulling back. "You look lovely yourself. Is this a new hat?"

Florence was a spunky older woman who never went anywhere without some type of head dress. Tonight's leopard-print cloche, set at a jaunty angle, went well with her brown top and matching brownstone jewelry.

"It's actually quite old, but I thought I'd bring it out for tonight's festivities. Can you believe our little Maxie is about to start his residency? It seems just the other day he started college."

Skye hid her smile. Maxwell would absolutely hate being called "little Maxie."

"I can't believe it. Time sure flies."

"I know. Feels like I just buried my second husband, but it's actually been fifteen years! Speaking of husbands, where is that husband of yours? I haven't seen him yet." Florence's eyes searched the room, and discomfort tightened Skye's chest.

"Do you mean Ethan?"

"Well, yes, dear. How many husbands do you have?" Amusement filled his aunt's voice.

Skye smiled politely. "He's here somewhere, but um... Ethan and I aren't married."

She hated how this conversation came up from time to time. Usually an older person in the family made the mistake, assuming she and Ethan were married because for years they saw her at all the family functions, right by Ethan's side—the way a wife would be.

Florence frowned in confusion. "What do you mean, you're not married? Of course you're married." Her eyes dipped to Skye's bare left hand. "Oh. I guess I'm getting old. I could have sworn you and my nephew were married. You're practically part of the family. What are you waiting for, dear?"

The tightness in her chest intensified, and Skye desperately wanted to escape the conversation. Instead, she said the practiced lie she used to save face.

"Ethan and I are happy the way we are. We don't need a piece of paper to define our relationship."

Florence harrumphed. "A piece of paper? Is that all you think it is? Let me tell you a secret. That piece of paper determines whether or not you have any rights regarding his money or property should something happen to him. Lock him down and get a ring on your finger before all your good years are gone. How old are you? Thirty-one, thirty-two?"

"Thirty-four."

Florence gasped, as if she'd told her she was nearing her seventy-fifth birthday. "Thirty-four? Your prime child-bearing years are almost gone. By the time I was your age, I already had three of my four children. You do want children, don't you?"

Heat flooded Skye's neck. She did, but that wasn't a conversation to have with Ethan's aunt. "Um..."

"Never you mind. You tell my nephew to piss or get off the pot, you hear me? He's so busy all the time, he'll probably delay getting married for another decade if you let him. You know what I did with my first husband? Gave him an ultimatum, and the next thing you know, bam. I had a ring. Sometimes they need a little nudge." She winked.

"I'll remember that," Skye said.

"Auntie Florence, what are you over here talking to Skye about?" Monica slipped an arm around Skye's shoulder.

"Giving her some much needed advice."

"Did she ask for advice?" Monica asked, resting a fist on her narrow hip.

Florence pursed her lips. "Why are you so rude, child? I'm convinced your mother brought home the wrong baby from the hospital."

Monica let out a loud laugh, and Skye covered her mouth as she quietly giggled.

"Auntie, that's mean."

Florence mumbled something and then looked Skye dead

in the eyes. "Remember what I said. Piss or get off the pot." She cast an annoyed look at Monica before sauntering away.

"*What* was that about?" Monica asked, eyes bright with mischief.

"She was giving me relationship advice." Skye grimaced.

"About you and Ethan?"

Skye nodded.

"Let me guess, she thinks you should be married by now."

Skye nodded again.

Monica sighed and said out the corner of her mouth, "I swear all these old ass people think about is marriage, marriage, marriage. Oh, and babies. They can't imagine some people are perfectly happy with the way their relationships are. I'm sorry you had to put up with her unsolicited advice." She lifted two colorful drinks from a server's tray. "Here. Enjoy. You've probably earned this. And come with me. Remember my cousin, Rene? She and a bunch of girlfriends stayed at the same villa you and Ethan rented in Italy two summers ago. She's been going on and on about it, and I told her you were coming tonight, so she wants to thank you for the rec."

Skye followed Monica across the room and greeted her cousin. While they talked, Ethan reentered the room and strolled over to where several men carried on a conversation.

She half-listened to Rene, all her attention focused on Ethan.

The lie she told his aunt slipped easily from her lips, but the truth was, she didn't know how Ethan felt about marriage. He seemed content with their relationship status, and a more permanent condition had never been hinted at, much less discussed.

She did know, however, that his first marriage ended in a messy divorce he refused to talk about in detail. She had broached the subject before, but each time, he shut her down within minutes. Whatever that woman did, she had scarred him.

Maybe she should try again, dig deeper into his first marriage.

Her feigned agreement with Monica's point of view was exactly that—feigned. She wanted to get married one day—ached for it. Lately, the desire to be Ethan's wife and an urge to be the mother of little Ethans and Skyes gnawed relentlessly at her. Ever since they celebrated seven years together six months ago, she hadn't been able to stop thinking about their future, and she wanted more. She wanted to celebrate wedding anniversaries, not dating anniversaries.

Maybe his aunt was right with her crude analogy.

Piss or get off the pot.

Chapter Three

As expected, Ethan found his mother in the kitchen directing the servers, who swept in with empty trays and out with the trays full of food and drinks. Almost every surface of the chef-style kitchen was covered with delicious options, like bruschetta with a balsamic reduction and buttery pastry squares filled with cheddar, spinach, and caramelized onions.

He picked up a square from a silver platter and slowly chewed, enjoying the burst of flavor across his tongue.

Leaning back against a long counter, Ethan folded his arms across his chest and crossed his right foot over the left at the ankles. "Mom, what are you doing in here? Bruno's staff has everything under control. Let them do their jobs."

The food was catered by his stepbrother's restaurant, and everything he tasted this evening had been delicious, which was no surprise. An added benefit to having his brother's company cater meant he could eat everything on the menu without worry, unlike when he attended other events. A severe shellfish allergy limited his options, and though there was no shellfish on the menu, Bruno would have made sure his cooks took extra precautions to avoid cross-contamination.

When he traveled, his personal assistant called ahead and reminded hotels about his allergy, and he was very selective about the restaurants he patronized. His diligence had paid off, and for years, he hadn't suffered from a major allergic reaction.

Rose Santana faced him, and her lips broke into a smile. Her skin was almost the same mahogany hue as his, but that's where the similarity ended. Ethan was over six feet tall like his father, while his mother was a petite, slender woman barely over five feet.

Her black hair, streaked with gray, was styled in a chignon and secured by a rhinestone hair pin embellished with white flowers at the end. A simple black dress skimmed her small frame and a lovely broach matching the clip in her hair added a touch of elegance.

"It's still my house and my party," she said.

"You work too hard."

"Well, if that's not the pot calling the kettle black." Rose walked over to stand beside him. "You look very handsome tonight."

He adored this woman. Before she met and married his stepfather, she'd worked hard to provide for him and his siblings after their father passed away. Being the oldest and stubborn, Ethan had been protective of his mother and protective of his father's memory. He could admit now that he'd been very difficult because he hadn't wanted to betray his father's memory. Eventually, his mother's love and his stepfather's patience wore him down, and he accepted their relationship.

"You always say that."

"Because you always look handsome. I like this red. I think it's adorable the way you and Skye find ways to match. Like the time you went to the awards banquet, and you both wore turquoise. You with the turquoise tie and her in that lovely turquoise gown. The photos from the event were gorgeous."

"That's all Skye. She likes that kind of thing."

"You should let her redesign your office. Add some color to that boring black and white."

"I happen to like the way my office is designed. I let Skye add her touches to the house, but I draw the line at my office space."

"As long as the two of you have been together, there should be no lines," his mother said, her voice heavy with meaning.

He knew what was coming next. "Don't start."

Rose rested a hand on his arm. "You should marry her. It's been long enough, and I want grandkids."

After he turned thirty-five last year, her complaints about the lack of grandchildren became more frequent. Most of the time she only dropped hints, but he figured her constant talking about grandchildren was because Maxwell would be moving out of state for his residency. Monica was the only one of her kids living at home, but his sister's busy social calendar meant frequent absences from home. His mother was probably starting to feel a heavy dose of empty nest syndrome.

"We don't have to be married to give you grandkids," Ethan pointed out.

"Then get started."

"You have three already," he reminded her, referring to his sister Audra's children.

She sent a reproachful look in his direction. "I would love to have more. No grandparent has ever said, 'No more grandchildren. I have enough.'"

"Don't look here because it's not happening anytime soon. Skye and I are happy the way we are."

"You're sure about that?" Rose asked.

The question triggered unease to skitter up his spine and

doubt filtered into his consciousness. A wrinkle creased their relationship lately. Nothing he could quite put a finger on, but Skye had changed. Some days she seemed distant, introspective. A few times he caught her staring at him, and when he asked what was wrong, she laughed and said she was just thinking about something.

"She hasn't said a word to me," he said.

Rose sighed dramatically.

One of the female servers approached. "Mrs. Santana, we're almost out of the finger sandwiches. We could make more or let them run out."

Rose assessed the contents of the kitchen. "We have plenty of food, so let them run out. But in thirty minutes, start pouring the champagne for the toast."

"Yes, ma'am."

After the young woman walked away, Rose moved to stand in front of her son. "You're not getting any younger."

"I'm thirty-six, not fifty-six. Men don't have the same reproductive concerns women do. I can have children well into old age."

"What about Skye? As you pointed out, her reproductive concerns are different."

This conversation was entering territory no one but him and Skye had any business traveling. Getting married and having children should be a private conversation, one that he and Skye had clearly decided they didn't need. Other than inquiring about his previous marriage a few times, Skye had never mentioned a desire to get married or have children. He was confident they were on the same page—more or less.

"And just because you can have kids later in life," his mother continued, "doesn't mean it'll be easy. Your sperm slows down and becomes less virile."

"My swimmers will be fine, mother dear. They are a very robust bunch."

"Yuck." Monica had entered the kitchen and approached with a wrinkled nose. "Please tell me when you say 'swimmers,' you mean fish."

Rose laughed. "Hi, honey."

Monica squeezed their mother from behind. "Hi, Mommy." She wasn't the youngest but acted like the baby of the bunch and was the closest one to their mother. She also hadn't truly decided on a career, unless one considered social media influencer a real job, which Ethan did not.

Rose patted the arm around her neck. "I'm giving your brother a hard time. He works too much and too hard."

"When did you cut off your hair?" Ethan asked his sister, in an effort to remove himself as the topic of conversation.

Monica ran a hand over her head. "Couple of weeks ago. If you followed my Instagram page like Skye does, you'd know that. What do you think? *Be nice.*"

"I like it."

She raised her eyebrows in disbelief. "Even though you prefer your women with hair?"

"My personal preference has nothing to do with you. The haircut really shows off your features."

Rose smiled softly at Monica. "I agree. Such pretty eyes and high cheekbones. She looks gorgeous."

Monica shrugged, pretending not to be pleased by the compliments. "It's just hair. If I change my mind, I can always grow it back. For now, this is me."

She lifted her ever present cell phone, positioned her body to show off the food in the kitchen, and snapped a selfie with puckered lips.

"Want a pic?" she asked Ethan.

"Do you want your phone smashed on the floor?"

"Ethan!" his mother admonished him.

He ignored her and shifted left so a male server could pick up a tray beside him.

"By the way, I need a favor," his mother began. "Your cousin, Nigel asked if—"

"No."

Monica snorted.

Rose pursed her lips at her daughter and then turned to Ethan. "You don't know what I'm going to say."

"I know exactly what you're going to say. You're going to ask me about a job for him. I'm not giving him a job or recommending him for one."

"Ethan, you're building a development worth billions. Surely you can find something for your cousin to do there."

"I've stuck my neck out for him enough. The last time I helped, he repaid me by having sex at his workplace."

"He said he apologized and felt terrible about it."

"He should. The woman he got caught with was the foreman's *wife*."

Monica gasped and broke out in a fit of giggles.

"Oh," Rose said, looking embarrassed. "He didn't mention that."

"I bet he didn't. Nigel will have to find his own jobs from now on." Ethan pushed away from the counter. "I'm going to mingle a little bit."

"You don't like mingling," Monica called after him.

She was right. He was like his mother in that way. His father had been the gregarious, outgoing one. The life of the party. The person whose arrival everyone looked forward to.

Rose preferred to be exactly where she was, in the background. His stepfather was similar to his father. He liked attention and could carry on a conversation with anyone. The man never met a stranger.

Back in the great room, Ethan remained on the outskirts of the group, and his eyes settled on Skye—a lovely standout in the room of sixty or so guests. She sat on the sofa, chatting with two of his female cousins.

She'd fit in right away with the Connor-Santanas, and over the years he liked to think they were essentially her family too.

Most of her family was still out west, in California. Her parents tragically passed away after a police chase ended in a multi-car pileup. The city compensated the families, and she received a sizable settlement at the young age of seventeen. She'd been on her own since then.

Despite the comments to his mother, Ethan did sometimes think about having children, but marriage was out of the question. He didn't need to be married. He and Skye had a good life together. They loved each other. They were comfortable. No piece of paper could make their bond any stronger.

Besides, he'd been burned once before and had no intention of going down the same path again.

Not even for Skye.

Chapter Four

The sound of someone tapping a fork against glass drew Skye's attention and halted the conversation she was having with a close family friend in the back. A hush fell over the room, and Benicio Santana went to stand in front of the fireplace.

Ethan's stepfather was originally from Mexico and for years worked in the entertainment industry, first as an actor and then as a director and producer. Swarthy-skinned with completely gray hair now, he hadn't lost any of his good looks and charm.

Benicio had built the sprawling mansion south of Atlanta to accommodate the blended family created when he married Ethan's mother. His stepfather had three boys, while his mother had come into the relationship with two girls and a boy. During the course of the marriage, the couple had Maxwell, the youngest in the family. The marriage lasted until three years ago when they amicably split but continued to celebrate holidays and milestones of their children together.

Ethan had told Skye more than once that he attributed his love for real estate and subsequent success to the nurturing he received from Benicio, as well as the investment the older man made in him from a very young age.

"Before the night is over, I want to take a moment to talk about my son, my youngest—the reason you are all here. Maxwell." Benicio's heavily accented voice brimmed with pride. He motioned for Maxwell to come forward, and the young man stepped away from a petite brunette, his date for the evening.

Leaning closer to Ethan, Skye asked, "Who is she?"

"I have no idea. I can't keep up with all his women," Ethan said.

Neither could Skye, and she almost felt sorry for the young woman. In a few months—possibly weeks—she would be replaced by another lovely young woman.

With toasty dark skin and too-long curly black hair, Maxwell was a blend of both his parents. He had his father's movie star looks and square jaw and his mother's dark eyes and cheekbones. A neat beard framed his mouth and made him look older than his twenty-six years.

Skye tuned back in to the wrap-up of Benicio's speech.

He placed a hand on his son's shoulder. "Rosa and I are very proud of this young man, and we appreciate all of you coming tonight to help us celebrate this milestone in his life."

"*Papi*, you're going to make me blush," Maxwell joked, and laughter rippled through the assembled guests.

"You deserve every compliment," Benicio said, very much the proud papa with his chest poked out and a grin encompassing his entire face. He rattled off a list of Maxwell's accomplishments, including his high score on the MCAT and his graduating magna cum laude. "If you have a drink, please join me in toasting to Maxwell—all he has done and all he has left to do."

Skye lifted her glass and joined in the cheers, smiling as

Maxwell gave his father a hug and then did the same to his mother standing nearby.

"My turn," Maxwell said.

Surprised murmurs went up from the crowd.

"Hey, it's my graduation party, right? I hadn't planned to say anything, but listening to my father made me realize how lucky I am. I couldn't have arrived at this point without the support of all of you, my family and friends. Especially my parents, of course, for encouraging me to pursue my passion instead of going into any one of my father's businesses. And you all had my back. A special shout out to my big brother Bruno who couldn't be here tonight. He regularly sent care packages, so I didn't have to worry about eating healthy. My roommates loved him."

Laughter erupted in the room.

"And another shout out to my other big brother, Ethan. Where is he?" His eyes searched the room until they landed on Ethan, and he grinned broadly. "Ethan, thank you for those conversations where you talked me down off the ledge. Your calm and words of wisdom helped me stay focused during the moments I doubted myself and thought about giving up. To his partner Skye, who I love like a sister, I'm sorry for all the late-night calls. I'm pretty sure I woke you up once or twice, but Ethan gives tough love like no one else I know. And I do mean tough."

More laughter. Because of the ten-year difference between them, at times Ethan behaved more like his father than an older brother.

Then the room fell quiet as Maxwell collected his thoughts.

"I guess that's all I have to say. Thank you all for coming tonight. I know I can handle the next stage of my life because I have a whole village behind me." He lifted his glass. "Cheers!"

"Cheers!" the crowd returned.

Tears welled in Skye's eyes. She always became emotional at events like this, and having Maxwell mention her name and talk about loving her like a sister made the emotion rise much faster and harder in her throat.

With no siblings of her own, she often felt alone in the world, and spending time with the Connor-Santanas filled the hole in her heart for a family. They treated her like part of the family, and she loved them.

But being treated like family and being part of the family were two different things. Maxwell had referred to her as Ethan's *partner*, but she secretly longed to be more.

She hated to be ungrateful because she was lucky. As far she knew, Ethan had been faithful to her all these years. To outsiders, he seemed cold and cutthroat, but he could be tender and was definitely generous. Those traits had ruined her for any other man.

When they were dining around town or flying to an exotic location, she convinced herself that her precarious state—simply being the girlfriend to a rich man—didn't matter. But it did matter, and she wanted more. Despite wanting more, she couldn't bring herself to walk away. How could she? When she essentially had everything she needed?

Almost.

There was definitely a restlessness in her of late, and Ethan's Aunt Florence had only highlighted what she'd been feeling for some time. A feeling of first-class seating on a train, speeding down a never-ending track to nowhere.

* * *

Skye stifled a yawn as she lounged in one of the chairs near the back of the room. Most of the guests were gone, but Benicio and two other people huddled nearby in conversation.

27

"You ready to go?" Ethan's voice was low in her ear as he bent over the back of the chair.

"Mhmm. I'm tired."

He came around and helped her to her feet.

They said goodbye to Benicio and the other guests and left the room hand in hand.

As they slipped out the door, his mother caught them. "You're not leaving, are you?" she asked.

"It's late," Ethan said.

"You shouldn't have to drive all the way out to your house at this time of night."

"Mom, I have a driver," he reminded her.

She pouted. "I know, but... why don't the two of you stay tonight? Audra and the kids are staying the night."

Audra, her oldest daughter, came into the hallway from the direction of the kitchen with Monica following close behind. Unlike Monica, she was short like their mother but had a more curvy figure.

"Hey, you aren't leaving, are you?" Audra asked.

"They are, but I'm trying to convince them to stay. In the morning, we can all have breakfast together," Rose said. She sounded so hopeful.

Monica flung her arm around her mother's shoulders. "I think that's a great idea."

Skye turned to Ethan, letting him make the decision on whether they should stay.

"We're going home. Another time," he said.

Crestfallen, Rose said, "Oh, all right."

They all hugged goodbye, and Ethan and Skye exited the house.

"Your mother was very disappointed we couldn't stay," Skye remarked.

"I know, but I have an early morning video meeting with

my Chinese partners. I can't stay here and lounge around like she wants us to."

"You're working tomorrow? It's Saturday."

"Unfortunately, I have no choice."

Ignacio, one of Ethan's stepbrothers, jogged up the stairs toward them. With his good looks and shoulder-length curly hair currently worn in a ponytail, he was quite the ladies' man.

"Good night, Ignacio," Skye said.

"Good night." He dropped a kiss on each of her cheeks. Unlike his father, he didn't have an accent because he arrived from Colombia at a young age, where he had lived with his mother after his parents divorced.

"I can't believe you don't have plans," Ethan said.

"Actually, I do have plans." Ignacio's eyes sparkled with mischief. "I'm leaving, but I forgot something in the house."

"You're leaving town tonight?" Skye asked in disbelief. He was in-between films, having flown from LA for Maxwell's graduation party.

"No, I'm staying for a few days."

"I'm sure Rose is happy. You're going to be spoiled."

"It's always good to be home, but I have a date tonight."

"A date?" Ethan repeated. "You've barely been in town twenty-four hours."

Ignacio shrugged with a wolfish grin. "You two should come with us. We're going to hit a club and have drinks, maybe do some dancing." He moved his hips suggestively.

"We're going home," Ethan said.

Ignacio shook his head. "You're like an old married couple."

He was joking, but the words sent a lance of pain through Skye's heart. Tonight was not her night.

"You two take care." Ignacio ran the rest of the way up the stairs, and she and Ethan entered the waiting limousine.

Chapter Five

"Everyone is gone."

Rose turned away from the dishes in the sink when she heard Benicio's voice. "I'm glad Ignacio was able to come. Too bad Thiago and Bruno couldn't make it."

"Bruno is in the middle of opening his new restaurant, and the flight from Brazil would be too long to justify Thiago coming for a party."

"He could have stayed a few days," Rose pointed out.

"Maybe. He really wanted to come but couldn't get away. Everything went well, though. You did a great job, as usual."

"It was fun, and Maxwell looked pleased."

During their marriage, whenever they entertained, they played to their strengths. She organized the events, while he made the rounds to ensure everyone was having a good time. As a former actor, he thrived in the spotlight and was simply better at engaging an audience. She loved to watch him "perform" with their guests, and over the years, he'd taught her a few tricks on how to be comfortable in large groups and overcome her introversion.

"Rosa, why are you doing that?" Benicio asked in a chiding voice, inclining his head toward the dirty dishes and leftover food. He'd always called her Rosa, from the moment they started dating. "You had hired help."

"I sent them home early. I needed something to keep me busy. I'm almost done."

"I will help you," he said.

"You don't have to," she said.

"I don't have to, but I will. What do you need me to do?"

Benicio loosened his cuffs and rolled up the sleeves to expose arms dusted with hair matching the white on his head. She missed running her fingers through the silky textured strands and sighing at the sensation of his soft beard against her neck. Those days were long gone.

"You're as bad as I am," Rose said good-naturedly.

They spent the next twenty minutes putting away the food, straightening the kitchen, and picking up stray cups and plates left at different places around the house. When they finished, they migrated to the living room, a much smaller space than the great room where guests spent most of their time during the party.

Rose eased onto the sofa and curled one leg beneath her, and Benicio relaxed in an armchair, long legs stretched out before him.

They sipped white wine, savoring the silence and camaraderie that came from years of knowing each other. Right from the beginning, she'd always been comfortable around Benicio, but she'd had reservations.

For one, they were so different. He was a Mexican businessman who started acting as a child and was worth hundreds of millions of dollars because of various business investments. She was a Black American woman who grew up on a farm and married young, struggling to raise three kids on her own after their father died.

At one point she lost her apartment and moved into a two-bedroom in a seedy neighborhood. Most nights she and the kids didn't sleep well because loud music constantly blared through the paper-thin walls or gunshots went off like firecrackers in the night.

Thank goodness for the financial and emotional support provided by her father and siblings, or she didn't know what she would have done to make ends meet. Two days after their little apartment got broken into and the few items of value she accumulated were stolen, Rose swallowed her pride and moved in with her brother and his wife.

Eventually she met Benicio but worried he didn't fully understand how much his life would change if he took on a ready-made family. At the time, his children lived in Colombia with their mother, who had taken them back to her home country after she and Benicio divorced. Then one day his ex-wife decided the boys should be with their father and sent them to the States. Suddenly, he was a single dad raising three boys under ten.

In bed one night, he proposed marriage, stating a practical reason for them to combine their households. His boys needed a mother figure, and her kids needed a father figure. As proposals went, it wasn't the most romantic, but she agreed. Two days later he gave her what he called a proper proposal, worthy of a woman of her caliber. The extravagant production was an over-the-top affair that included fireworks, a choir, and a horse drawn carriage. It was probably more for him than her, but she couldn't help but laugh and cry at the same time.

They married at a church downtown, not knowing she was pregnant with Maxwell, who arrived seven months after they tied the knot.

Friends and family jokingly referred to them as the Brady Bunch. It hadn't been easy blending households and cultures, but they made it work—until they couldn't anymore.

"Do you need help taking the gifts upstairs?" Benicio asked, his gray-eyed gaze drifting to the pile of envelopes and gift-wrapped boxes.

"I'll have Giselle take them upstairs in the morning," Rose said, referring to one of the younger members of the small household staff. Most days they were her only company. "I'm thinking about selling the house," she said quietly.

Startled, Benicio sat forward. "Why?"

"It's too much house now," she answered with a shrug. "Our kids are all adults with their own lives. Maxwell has had his own apartment for years, and once he starts his residency out of state, I'll never see him. Monica lives here, but she comes and goes as she pleases. Sometimes I don't see her for days."

"That may be, but we both know she's not going anywhere for a while."

"No, she's not."

They enjoyed a brief moment of laughter.

Rose stared down into her glass of wine but felt Benicio's gaze on her.

"We built this place together, Rosa. We designed it, picked out all the furniture and everything inside. You can't move. There are too many memories here. If you buy a smaller place, where will we host events like tonight?"

"We could rent space," Rose said.

"It's not the same, and you know that. What about Thanksgiving and Christmas? And your garden, hmm? You are going to give that up? Keep the house." He spoke with finality, as if the decision had been made simply because he said so.

"Since it's so great, how about I move out and you move back in?" Rose asked.

A beat passed.

"Because it would not be the same without you."

Her throat tightened with emotion, and Rose dipped her gaze to the wineglass as heaviness filled her heart. She felt the same. The house wasn't the same, not only because the kids were gone, but because Benicio was no longer there. She didn't dare utter those words because her ex-husband wouldn't let up if he suspected how she felt. She had to let him believe her decision to divorce him was the right one. She swallowed a mouthful of wine in the awkward silence.

Benicio drained his glass and set it on a table. "I should go. It's late." He made a point of looking at his watch.

Rose nodded and stood. "Where's your jacket and tie?"

"Around here somewhere."

They found them in the great room. He slipped his arms through the sleeves of the jacket and tucked the tie into one of the pockets.

They walked to the double doors.

"Do not make any hasty decisions about the house, okay?"

"I won't. I'll consult you first," Rose assured him.

"*Gracias.*"

Before he exited, they hugged, and she squeezed him a bit closer than she probably should, indulging in a whiff of his scent before they released each other.

"Drive carefully. Text me when you get home."

"*Sí, señora,*" he teased.

"Don't be difficult, Ben. Do as I say, please."

He laughed. "Don't I always? Good night, *mi amor.*"

"Good night."

Rose watched him walk into the dark to one of the few cars left in the driveway. Less than a minute later, the sight of his rear lights driving off the property hollowed her out, leaving her empty and forlorn at the demise of their marriage. Benicio should be joining her upstairs instead of going off to a separate home, but there was nothing she could do.

Their time had come and gone. Sometimes love wasn't enough.

Chapter Six

Something was wrong.

Skye hadn't been herself since they left the party.

Usually she let Ethan work undisturbed in the car, but he wasn't working, and she hadn't said a word in the past fifteen minutes. She crossed her legs away from him, one hand on her thigh, the other on the seat beside her, her head turned to look out the window at the nighttime scenery of buildings and cars whizzing by on the highway.

He'd noticed the same behavior before over the past few months—a certain withdrawal came and went with little explanation, and he could no longer ignore the signs of discontent. Time to find out exactly what the hell was going on.

He pressed the button to raise the privacy glass between them and Halston. "You've been quiet since we left the party. Did something happen that I need to know about?"

Her eyes met his in the dark interior. "No. I have a few things on my mind, that's all."

"Work?"

Skye worked at a community center providing after school care for kids in a low-income neighborhood.

"Yes. Thinking about the to-do list I have when I go in on Monday."

Her answer didn't ring true, and he hated lying.

"If there was something wrong, you'd tell me, wouldn't you?"

"*Yes.*" She sounded annoyed.

What the hell had he done? Nothing he could think of.

That was the problem with women. They could be silently seething and never express the emotion openly until one day they suddenly snapped. He knew all about that from his first wife, Joanne.

His skin crawled. Why the hell was he thinking about that venomous bitch? She and Skye were nothing alike. He and Skye meshed. She was calm and his family loved her. He liked coming home to her after a trip away. He liked talking to her on the phone. She was the perfect companion for family events and whenever they went out for a night on the town.

He loved her too. Everything about her. The way she talked, the way she laughed, the way she dressed, and the way she looked at him with adoration in her eyes, making him feel like a king among men.

That didn't mean she couldn't change, but he hadn't seen any behavior to suggest she was anything like his ex. The signs about Joanne had been there long before she showed her true nature. He'd simply ignored them.

He took Skye's hand. "Come sit next to me."

"Ethan..."

He gave a gentle tug, shutting down her refusal.

She hesitated, lips tightening, but then she slid across the leather seat, and he draped an arm across her shoulders.

"You obviously need to talk about whatever is on your

mind." He'd rather get the issues out in the open so they didn't fester and reemerge days later.

"It's nothing. I'll figure it out," Skye said quietly.

Ethan didn't push and kept her close to his side for the rest of the ride.

When they arrived at the mansion, she exited the car as soon as Halston opened the door. Ethan watched her almost race into the house without waiting for him or saying a word to Halston, which wasn't like her.

"Good night," he said to his driver.

"Good night, sir."

Ethan took the stairs to the bedroom they shared. Skye was in the process of removing her heels, standing by the king bed with her back to him.

"How much longer do I have to put up with your attitude?" he asked evenly, depositing his jacket on the cream-colored upholstered bench at the end of the bed.

He'd never had one of those until Skye became a fixture in his home. She'd made quite a few changes when she did.

The spacious, L-shaped bedroom contained a sitting room on the shorter section of the L, where a skylight and the large, overstuffed chairs Skye ordered added color in a previously empty space devoid of warmth after his ex-wife took the furniture. Now shelves of books turned the spot into a place for him to relax and read. Sometimes they ate breakfast at the round table near the French doors or outside on the wraparound balcony.

"I don't have an attitude," Skye said.

"I know you, Skye. You have an attitude."

She turned to face him and took a deep breath, releasing it with exaggerated force. "I want to talk to you about something."

Finally, progress. "Go ahead."

Ethan removed his cufflinks and placed them on a table,

next to a vase of peonies. Several feet away from Skye, he waited to hear her thoughts.

"Where do you see our relationship going?"

"I don't understand the question."

"I mean..." She swallowed.

Clear as day, unease surfaced in her face, and his stomach tightened as he anticipated her next words.

"Do you ever think about getting married again?" she asked.

"No."

Her eyes widened. "Just like that? No."

He shrugged. "You asked a question, I answered."

"So... you don't want to get married again, or you don't want to get married to me?"

"I have no interest in getting married again. You know how my last marriage ended."

"No, I don't, actually, because you never talk about it. You and Joanne have been divorced for eleven years. Are you really never going to marry again because of a relationship that ended when you were twenty-five years old?"

"What brought this on?" Had his mother been right? Had he been oblivious to Skye's deep desire for marriage?

"What brought this on?" she repeated angrily, removing her gold earrings with jerky movements. "I guess I don't want to hear anymore jokes about us being an old married couple—even if they are only jokes. I don't want another person in your family to ask me if I'm your wife and then have to explain that I'm not."

"Who the hell asked if you were my wife?"

"Your Aunt Florence referred to you as my husband. I corrected her, but it wasn't the first time someone in your family has said something similar to me."

"I've heard those comments too, and I ignore them. Besides,

Aunt Florence is old. Consider her absentmindedness a compliment. It means she sees you as part of the family."

"I'm not part of the family because we're not married."

Irritated, Ethan's jaw stiffened. "That's not true, and you know it. You're more a part of my family than any woman I've ever been involved with before, including my ex-wife. My family didn't warm up to her. My siblings adore you, and my parents think you're wonderful. You attend every family function with me. You *are* part of my family."

"Based on your terms."

"What does that mean?" Ethan demanded.

"I want to be part of your family on *my* terms, and those include a marriage license and a ring."

"When did you start wanting marriage?"

"I've always wanted to be married. I thought we'd get there eventually, but now you're saying marriage is completely out of the question."

"We've lived together for years and share our life together. The word wife is a title. It doesn't mean anything."

"If it doesn't mean anything, then why not give me the title?"

"You know why!" Ethan snapped.

"Because Joanne is the devil."

"Yes," he said between teeth tightly pressed together.

They stared at each other until the silence stretched between them to an uncomfortable level.

"You don't trust me, and you believe whatever Joanne did to you, I'll do too. I'm being punished for her sins."

"I'm not punishing you. Everything you ask me for, I give you. You have credit cards for shopping and a closet filled with designer dresses and shoes, fine jewelry, accessories. You have full control of the house, take spa days whenever you want, and travel to exotic vacations to parts of the world some people have never heard of. You're telling me that isn't enough? Do you want the blood from my veins?" He held out his wrists to her. "Will that be enough for you?"

A glimmer of pain stole across her face. "I'm not sure you have any blood in your veins. That would mean you have a heart."

He laughed bitterly. "You're letting a few words said in passing spoil our evening."

"The way I feel didn't start tonight. I've felt this way for a while. I wish I'd..."

His ears pricked up, eyes zeroing in on her expression to read her mind.

"What did you say?" he asked slowly. She broke eye contact. "Finish the sentence!" he barked.

Skye jumped. He seldom raised his voice.

Her eyes met his again, this time with defiance. "I wish I'd known you felt this way. I would have made different choices."

Her words landed with the force of a thunderbolt and charged the air around them.

Then she brushed past him on the way to her dressing room.

Chapter Seven

E than caught Skye's wrist and pulled her around to face him.

Speaking in a measured tone, he said, "I hope you're not thinking of doing something foolish, like leaving me."

She'd been slipping away for a while, and the sensation of loss flourished tonight, beating down on him with relentless fists.

"Why would I leave when I have so much? Everything a woman could want."

Her posture and expression suggested the complete opposite of the words coming out of her mouth. Blatant antagonism hardened her lush lips, and a spark of fury lit her eyes as she challenged him with direct eye contact. This wasn't the Skye he knew. Biting sarcasm and flashes of anger intruded into a relationship which, for the most part, had been filled with white hot passion and enjoyable companionship.

Skye yanked away her arm and went into her dressing room, slamming the door and shutting him out.

What the hell was going on?

She'd essentially admitted the mysterious undercurrent of discontent he had sensed was dissatisfaction with their relationship status. She must have been thinking about leaving him all along, and his refusal of marriage might be the catalyst for her to walk out the door.

Ethan experienced a knee-jerk rejection at the notion of Skye abandoning their life together. She was his, ring or not, and leaving him meant leaving his home and heart empty.

"We should talk about this," Ethan said.

"There is nothing to talk about. You've made your position clear," Skye called through the door.

Ethan ran a weary hand over his head. He didn't need conflict right now. He didn't need conflict ever. For the most part, he and Skye enjoyed an easy-going relationship with few disagreements. When they did argue, jewelry or some other expensive trinket helped resolve their issues. He doubted a necklace would be the answer to tonight's problem.

Skye came out of the closet with her hair down and wearing a sheer, pale-pink nightgown. The thing was almost see-through, presenting her dark nipples and areola through the thin material. He almost replaced the urge to finish the conversation with a crawl between the sheets, deep languid sucks on her lush breasts, and the inevitable slide between her soft thighs for relief.

But he had work to do, and she wouldn't let him touch her. He was almost certain she'd worn that nightgown on purpose. Forcing him to stand there with his hands in his pockets, like a good little boy who had been warned about reaching into the cookie jar.

Ethan sighed. "Good night."

Skye pulled the bed linens over her body. "Good night," she said, voice below freezing.

He walked over to the bed and looked deeply into her eyes.

"I love you." Perhaps a reminder of the depth of his feelings would be enough.

Her cool mask fell away and exposed a vulnerability he'd never seen before, and guilt spiraled in his gut.

"I love you too, Ethan," she whispered.

He kissed her forehead and then went into his dressing room and changed into a pair of pajama bottoms. Before leaving, he took one last glance at Skye, the tempting vision she made with her eyes closed, lying in his bed where she belonged. He couldn't imagine not having her there.

He turned out the light and went downstairs to his office.

Once inside, Ethan sat at his desk in the dark, a glass of whiskey in hand. He swirled the amber liquid and took a sip. Outside the window, bright light suddenly illuminated the expansive grounds when the motion sensors picked up on Mona, his housekeeper, walking to her apartment in the carriage house.

He should be prepping for his meeting but couldn't think. Now he understood the odd strain between him and Skye, where one minute everything was fine, and the next she was giving him the silent treatment.

She wanted marriage.

He loved to spoil her, and in the beginning of their relationship, she used to be overwhelmed by his gifts. She would scream and clap and do a little dance. Hug him and kiss him, and one time she cried. He hadn't received such an exuberant response in a long time.

Nowadays when he gave her a gift, she seemed... bored. The gifts were bigger and grander, but her reactions remained muted.

He swore softly.

Marriage.

She'd blindsided him. He didn't want or expect to get married again.

Before Skye came into his life, he'd been sowing his wild oats after the end of his marriage, avoiding monogamy but open and upfront with all his lovers. Most women didn't care. They appreciated his candor and simply expected a good time until they went their separate ways. A few had been hurt when they developed feelings and realized he had no intention of getting serious.

Then he met Skye at the bar of The Rose Hotel, his first hotel acquisition and renovation, which he'd named after his mother. She'd been stood up by a blind date, and the other man's loss was his gain.

He'd intended for their hook up to be a one-night stand, but one night turned into two, and two nights turned into a week. The next thing he knew, he was in a committed relationship and introducing Skye to his family. The progression of their relationship happened fast, but it felt right.

Within months of dating, he couldn't deny Skye's importance to him, and those feelings only intensified over time. He loved her, but he had no intention of being a fool again. His first marriage had ended in disaster, and because of such a painful experience, there were certain lines he didn't cross—wouldn't cross. Not even for Skye.

The tension in their relationship would eventually pass. She was suffering from a case of the seven-year itch, that's all. For now, he'd be patient and pay attention to her moods.

But he would not allow her to strong arm him into marriage.

Chapter Eight

Inside her dressing room, Skye padded on bare feet across the floor as she perused the racks of clothes. Ethan might be indifferent to her feelings about marriage, but she couldn't accuse him of being stingy.

Designer clothes and shoes accumulated during their years together filled her closet. Soft white rugs partially obscured the ebony floors and matched the white shaker cabinets containing cashmere sweaters, tailored slacks, and other high-end clothing. Inside the drawers of the center island, more high-quality items resided—belts, scarves, and hair accessories.

The less expensive pieces mixed in were pieces she had purchased from time to time at department stores or off the discount rack at high-end retailers. Most of the items, however, were expensive gifts from Ethan or had been bought with a card he'd given her that was attached to one of his accounts.

"Ready to go?" His voice came from outside the closet.

"Almost." Not exactly true. She currently wore a pair of beige panties and the matching lace-cupped bra.

They were meeting two friends at Rico's, a trendy restaurant in Midtown known for its vast Sunday brunch menu and kick-ass mimosas. She and Ethan hadn't seen the other couple for months, ever since Amy gave birth to twins. Before that, the couples saw each other several times a year at parties and get-togethers, and one time took a short vacation to the beach with two other couples.

Amy had been the one to call and invite them to brunch, her voice furtive and desperate as she pleaded with Skye to make time, because she needed a break and an excuse to get out of the house. Brian topped Ethan's list of preferred real estate attorneys, and they had developed a friendship outside of their business relationship.

Leaving her hair down in loose curls, Skye pulled on a colorful off-the-shoulder dress and added knee-high gold boots that showed through the side split when she walked. She searched the shelves of designer purses and settled on a small black one with a gold handle which she stuffed with her ID and other items.

She turned out the light and stepped out of the closet in time to catch Ethan glancing at his watch. Freshly shaved, his aftershave drifted on the air in the several feet separating them. A gentle ache surfaced between her thighs at the familiar smell. Instinctively, she wanted to rub the back of her hand over his smooth jaw and kiss him. They hadn't kissed in what seemed like ages, and she missed the warm press of his mouth to hers and the teasing way he always tugged her lower lip between his teeth. But she refrained. After Friday night's conversation, an odd tension buzzed between them, unlike any type of friction she'd ever experienced with him before.

Usually, they argued and one or the other eventually apologized. Ethan often gave her a gift of some kind—a pair of earrings, a tennis bracelet, a nice purse, or something equally expensive. Then the moment passed. This time, neither had apologized, and the unease remained between them like a thin veil, though they behaved as if everything was normal.

"I'm ready," Skye announced.

Ethan assessed her appearance. His dark, hungry gaze glided over the way her hair tumbled onto her bare shoulders and how the loose fit of the dress seemed to enlarge her ample breasts and hips. He licked his lips—she didn't think he even knew he'd done it—and her nipples turned into hard, aching points, longing for the stroke of his tongue. That talented tongue of his was a dangerous weapon, designed to give a woman extraordinary pleasure. On more than one occasion, his dark head between the golden pillars of her thighs had so stimulated her arousal, she'd come from the mere sight of him eating her out.

He turned abruptly away. "Let's go," he said, in a rough voice.

Skye's shoulders slumped. They were definitely in an odd place. Ethan never resisted the urge to touch her.

Today was Halston's day off. Instead of calling the car service he often used when Halston was unavailable, Ethan was driving to the restaurant in one of his other vehicles.

While Skye waited at the front door, body humming from the sexually charged moment in the bedroom, he pulled into the circular driveway in the Rolls-Royce Phantom, which he had purchased only last year for an obscene amount. The base price alone had been close to half a million dollars, but Ethan worked with the bespoke team to add additional touches which increased the price tag. The most obvious of which was the unique gray color the manufacturer mixed for the exterior. If another buyer requested the same shade, the company needed Ethan's permission to sell it.

Riding in the Phantom was an experience of extravagant touches like soft gray leather seats, lamb's wool floor mats, and a computerized dashboard. The virtually soundproof car included a starlight headliner, which were intricate fiber optic roof lights that re-created the charm of a star-speckled sky.

They didn't say much to each other for the first few minutes of the ride, but when they stopped at a traffic light, Skye decided to make an effort to break the uncomfortable silence.

"How are things going with Horizon?" she asked.

"We're a little behind schedule but making progress. The designers met with me and my team to present ideas for phase two. We're still debating the benefits and drawbacks to the various models, but I told my team to make a decision by the middle of the week so we can move forward. I'm going down there tomorrow to check on the progress."

To light a fire under them, no doubt, Skye thought. "I guess the China meeting went well?"

Ethan grunted. "The project is a pain in my side."

The sound of sirens pierced the almost soundproof interior of the car, and Skye tensed, a reaction she wished to no longer experience but held no control over.

Ethan reached for her left hand and squeezed, and the comforting gesture lowered the rate of her racing heart. He knew what the sound of sirens did to her. He and Halston understood if she was in the car, they stopped immediately and did not move until they knew where the emergency vehicle was and it passed.

Skye had been in the car with her parents when the accident happened. They were running late to meet friends for dinner and planned to attend a movie afterward. Her father had heard the siren but didn't know where the sound was coming from. Not behind him, certainly. He eased into the intersection, and the police cruiser T-boned them.

She lost two weeks of her life, waking up from an induced

coma with broken bones and damaged insides. Ultimately, she survived the wreckage. Her parents did not.

Two police cars whizzed by in front of them, and only after they passed was she able to breathe easier. She took deep, calming breaths—a trick a therapist taught her. The exercise helped, but having Ethan hold her hand helped more.

At least her reaction wasn't as bad as before, when she used to freeze and hyperventilate. She'd come a long way in the years since the accident.

Ethan gave her hand one more squeeze before continuing the drive to the restaurant.

Once they arrived, Rico, the owner, greeted them at the entrance. "Ethan, it's been a long time." A large man, Rico stood several inches above Ethan with big meaty hands and a round middle.

"Too long," Ethan agreed, shaking his hand.

"Hello, Skye, looking lovely as always," Rico said.

"Thank you." She lifted her cheek for an air kiss from him.

He picked up two menus and personally escorted them toward their table.

Walking behind both men, Skye caught the surreptitious glances of various women as Ethan passed. He was certainly tall, dark, and handsome, striking an imposing image of smooth confidence in mud brown slacks and a tan long-sleeved shirt.

As they approached the table where their friends sat, Brian stood to greet them.

"I was worried you weren't coming," he said. His brown hair lay in perfect waves, as usual.

"And pass up a free meal at Rico's? You don't know me very well," Ethan said.

Skye joined in the laughter that erupted, genuinely pleased to be in the company of other people, instead of having to endure the stilted conversation she and Ethan experienced in the car.

Hugging her friend Amy, a perky blonde with waist length hair and sparkling, friendly eyes, she said, "Blame it on me. I was running a little late."

"We already knew you were at fault. Ethan's way too prompt for your tardiness to have been his fault," Brian teased.

Skye pointed a finger at him. "I'm going to let your comment pass—this time," she said, and they all laughed again.

Ethan pulled out her chair, and she sat down. He sat to her left.

After the waitress took their orders, Skye said, "Well, I guess I don't have to ask what you two have been up to."

A knowing look passed between the couple.

"It's been quite an experience," Amy said.

"Everything changes in your life. And I mean *everything*." Brian squeezed lemon juice into his water. "Listen, we don't want to bore you with talk about babies and staying up all night. We invited you to brunch because we want to avoid all that. The grandparents are on babysitting duty, so we have a chance to relax for a few hours and be grown-ups for the first time in months."

"He talks as if he hasn't been going to work," Amy said with an eye roll.

"With two more mouths to feed, you can't really blame me." Brian covered his wife's hand with his. "But I admit, Amy's had the worst of it. Thank goodness our moms have taken turns helping us. I don't know how single parents do it."

The conversation shifted to news about mutual friends, and Ethan brought them up to speed on Maxwell's graduation party and his plans to go out of state for his residency.

He appeared so at ease as he talked to their friends, laughing as if he didn't have a care in the world. As if she imagined the tension between them, like she had imagined their relationship was on a different, deeper level than the reality.

Was she imagining the tension between them? Maybe Ethan had already moved past their argument. Meanwhile, she couldn't stop thinking about their future together. Had she wasted the past seven years? Should she leave him now, instead of wasting another seven years or more?

Halfway through brunch, Amy said, "Oh, did you hear? Erica and Tom are getting a divorce."

"Babe." Brian's deep frown clearly signaled she should be quiet.

Amy tossed her hair. "It's true."

"You don't know that," Brian said in a harder tone.

"The man packed up his belongings and *moved out*, Brian." She returned her attention to Ethan and Skye. "Can you believe it? After fifteen years, they're throwing in the towel." Amy shook her head and cut into what was left of her stack of pancakes.

"Any idea why?" Skye asked.

Amy always knew the latest about everyone. Even when pregnant and bedridden, when Skye called to check on her, she knew the scoop about their friend circle better than Skye did. She was convinced Amy had placed listening devices in all her friends' homes.

"No, we don't know why," Brian replied in the same hard tone.

Amy ignored him. "Rumors of infidelity, on both their parts. I guess we'll find out for sure once the divorce proceedings start." She sipped her mimosa and arched an eyebrow.

"Proof that getting married is no indication of a relationship's success," Ethan said.

Skye stiffened. That unnecessary comment had to be for her benefit.

Amy nodded. "True. I—"

"Getting married can, however, be an indication of a couple's commitment to each other." Skye stabbed a sausage link with her fork and bit off a piece.

"Commitment is in the heart and demonstrated through actions." Ethan cast a sidelong glance at her.

"Some people need more, and if the love is real, marriage wouldn't be too much to ask."

"And some people are never satisfied," Ethan said evenly.

Skye almost choked on the hurtful words. He thought she wasn't *satisfied*?

A hush fell over the table as she and Ethan eyed each other.

She dropped her gaze first, picking up her glass of water and taking a sip to cool the burn of being humiliated in front of their friends.

Amy cleared her throat. "Oh! I need to show you pictures of the boys. We hired a photographer to take professional photos."

"Yes, show them the pictures," Brian said, glancing nervously between Skye and Ethan.

Amy whipped out her phone, probably the worst thing that could happen after the tense moment between Skye and Ethan. Skye didn't want to look at pictures of babies when she might never have any of her own.

The more she thought about Ethan's words, the more her blood boiled. She didn't give a damn about Erica and Tom or any other failed marriage.

She would never have what Brian and Amy did. It was almost as if the universe were conspiring to make sure she knew what she was missing. For years, she never paid much attention to other people's relationships. But once the seed of longing was planted, the harvest was bountiful. Like having purchased a white car and suddenly seeing white cars everywhere, she couldn't escape conversations about marriage and babies.

All she saw were happy couples. The ring on Amy's finger drew her eye. So did the couple in the corner, leaning across the table to speak to each other in conspiratorial tones. She couldn't miss the older couple dining with what looked like their grandchildren.

All of it, all of them, were glaring symbols of what was missing in her life.

Symbols of what she would never have with the man she loved—a man who claimed to love her.

Chapter Nine

Skye pulled her Lexus into a parking space outside the one-story brick building of the Decatur Student Learning Center. Working at the center was a labor of love. The pay wasn't very good, but because of the settlement she received after her parents were killed, she could afford to do something she loved, which was help kids.

She and two other employees organized volunteers who worked with the children every school day. They helped with homework, taught them to grow food in the community garden, and encouraged extra-curricular activities like sports and acting.

Employees often filled in where needed. Some days Skye worked in the office doing filing, answering the phone, or greeting children as they came through the door. Other days she worked in a classroom when one of the tutors was out, or she drove a van to pick up the children from the neighboring schools to bring them here.

She punched in her code at the door, and the lock clicked open.

They were fortunate to have this space. One day she had remarked to Ethan that she wished they had a bigger facility to accommodate the need in the community. They'd had to turn some parents away, and the waiting list grew longer each semester.

A week later, he showed her this building. At the time, it needed work but was in an up-and-coming neighborhood, and she saw the potential. The main building could house the office and some of the classrooms, while the buildings in the back could be used for additional classrooms and a recreation area.

To her surprise, Ethan renovated the building at no cost to the organization. He also convinced one of his contacts who owned a security company to install a high-end system. In exchange, Ethan promised to do future business with him. He then practically donated the buildings and land, selling them for a fraction of their worth. The low mortgage allowed the center to provide additional programs and supplies for the children.

That meant better snacks and more extra-curricular activities, like art classes offered by local artists who donated their time to teach the kids. A retired football player, whom everyone called "Coach," ran around the yard with them every day. They played football, kickball, jumped rope, and anything else he deemed helpful to give them exercise before they buckled down on their school work.

The employees worked at the very front in a wide open room. File cabinets, three desks, and bulletin boards overrun by colorful papers pinned to the cork board surfaces were crammed into the space.

Thresa Davis waved from her desk in the corner as Skye came in. "Hey, lady," she called.

Skye placed her purse in her desk drawer. "Hi. Where's

Janelle?" She was running late, so Janelle should have been there already.

"Called and said she couldn't come in today. Had to get her hair and nails done and buy a new outfit for a big date with her boyfriend." Thresa shrugged.

"*Okay*. It's just the two of us, then. Not so bad."

Skye couldn't hide her grin, and Thresa grinned back.

Janelle didn't fit in with them, and work went more smoothly when she wasn't around. She'd worked at the center for six months but still became confused with the simplest tasks. Worse than that, she was sometimes rude to Thresa and Skye and often complained about the kids and their parents.

She was nothing like Thresa. Thresa enjoyed working with children and used to spend a lot of her time and resources helping them by volunteering at various non-profits. After twenty-seven years, she retired from UPS but wanted to stay busy. She started working at the center a couple of years ago. They'd been good friends ever since.

Skye went over to Thresa's desk and perused her basket of goodies. She always had something yummy to snack on—chocolate, cookies, cakes.

She found two Hershey's kisses, opened one, and popped it in her mouth. "How are the grandkids?" she asked.

A bright smile spread across Thresa's face. With golden, wrinkle-free skin and long dark hair in a single braid down her back, she didn't look like someone with five adult children and two grandkids.

"A mess. We Face-Timed last night. They want me to come for Christmas, but I'm not sure. We'll see."

Like Skye, Thresa used to live in California.

"You should go. Things slow down around the holidays anyway because the students are out of school for a couple of weeks. We'll be fine without you."

"*We?* Don't you mean *you?*"

Skye snickered and went back to her desk. "I guess so because I won't be getting much help from our co-worker, will I?"

"No, you won't."

Settling into her chair, Skye said, "But at least there'll be less work. I shouldn't get overwhelmed."

"The holidays are a few months away. I have time to make a decision and let you know if you'll need to cover for me. How was the graduation party?"

"Very nice."

Skye launched into an explanation with full detail about the food and the guests. A few times the phone ringing interrupted them, and at one point a tutor came in early to drop off some materials for later.

When she was finished, Thresa sighed. "They do everything on a grand scale, don't they?"

"Always," Skye confirmed.

In the past, she'd shown Thresa pictures of other parties she attended with Ethan.

"So, do I get to meet your man in a couple of weeks? He's coming to the play, isn't he?" Thresa stapled a stack of papers.

"I'm not sure. His work is so unpredictable. He says he's coming, but anything could happen with one of his deals, and then he might have to stay late and miss the whole event."

"I hope he can come. He's practically the reason all of this is possible."

The Decatur Student Learning Center was not a priority for the executive director. He worked in a separate office managing two other nonprofits, which meant she, Thresa, and Janelle practically worked autonomously. As long as the office ran smoothly in this location, he could spend time schmoozing donors for his more high-profile organizations. Sometimes, Skye wondered if he'd forgotten they existed.

"I'll talk to Ethan, but I can't make any promises."

* * *

Skye found Ethan in his home office. The door was ajar, so she knocked twice and pushed it open. He glanced up from behind the large desk when she walked in.

The awkwardness between them had intensified since Sunday brunch with Brian and Amy. After she and Ethan traded words, the other couple spent the rest of the meal trying to ease the tension by good-naturedly complaining about sleepless nights and lack of alone time, in addition to showing them photos and twenty-second videos of their "adorable little monsters."

Yesterday evening, Ethan worked late in his home office and skipped dinner. By the time he came to bed, Skye was lying on her side pretending to be asleep. Although she sometimes scooted over to his side to experience the warm comfort of skin-to-skin contact, they were past the stage in their relationship where they cuddled every night.

Within minutes, he was snoring gently beside her, sleeping fitfully while she lay wide awake, unable to slow the thoughts marching back and forth through her head.

The argument might be in the past, but the strain it placed on their relationship remained ever present.

"Are you still planning to come to the play at the center?" Skye asked.

"When is it?" Ethan sat back in the chair.

"At seven." She gave him the date. "Shouldn't last more than thirty minutes, and afterward, we have refreshments for the kids and the audience. I only mention it because Thresa's looking forward to meeting you, and I think you should see the results of everything you've done for us."

"I didn't do much except sell you a building."

"Completely renovated, at a fraction of its value. I've told you before, but the savings allowed us to provide additional services for the children. You should come."

"I'll do my best to make it."

"Thank you."

She hesitated in the doorway, wanting to say more but not knowing what to say. She could hardly stand the distance between them. The crack in their union was spreading, driving them further apart, and slowly tearing *her* apart. She needed to talk to Ethan about her feelings, but his expression wasn't welcoming, and she knew where he stood—in direct opposition to her.

"Are you going to stay down here much longer?"

"At least another hour." No emotion crossed his face.

He spoke to her like he might speak to a stranger, and she couldn't help but wonder if he was avoiding her.

Sometimes when he worked at the house, she'd curl up on the sofa opposite his desk simply to be near him—reading a magazine or the latest women's fiction novel. When he finished, they'd climb the stairs together and go to bed. If he finished early, they'd make a snack in the kitchen and go to the theater room to watch a movie. None of which was going to happen tonight. The crack was too wide, and right now, she didn't feel welcomed in his immediate space.

"Did you eat?" she asked, needlessly prolonging the conversation.

"Daria ordered dinner for me before I left work. I ate there." His voice remained monotone, lifeless.

"All right. Well... I'll probably be asleep when you come up. Good night."

She hesitated, but he immediately returned his attention to the papers on his desk. Skye swallowed the pain of his dismissal and slipped out of the office, returning the door to the same position in which she found it.

Their conversation didn't sound normal, their voices injected with a faux-casualness any hearing person could catch —a far cry from how they usually behaved. No more teasing banter. No more sexual innuendo.

As far as she could remember, they'd never gone this long with tension between them.

In the space of only days, their once passionate affair was barely chugging along on fumes, teetering on the edge of extinction. At least in her mind. Ethan might not view their interactions in the same light.

If she were being honest, the fault of their relationship woes lay squarely on her shoulders. Ethan had never made false promises or misled her, but finding out he was completely opposed to marriage had devastated her.

She hadn't realized how much she'd wanted to be his wife until the possibility had been taken away.

Chapter Ten

P hone pressed to his ear, Ethan reclined in his chair and listened to Suzanne update him on the China project. Outside the window, Atlanta buildings reach toward the sky, but his was the tallest on the block and allowed him to see for miles.

"So far, so good," Suzanne said, wrapping up. "I don't think you have anything to worry about—for now." Her British-accent voice—crisp and clear—conveyed efficiency.

A note from Daria popped up in the chat box on his computer. *Your stepfather is here.*

Although he had a busy schedule, he always made time for family.

"Suzanne, I have an unexpected visitor. If that's all..."

"Yes, absolutely. I'll be in touch if anything changes."

They ended the call, and Ethan typed a response in the chat box. *Send him in.*

Seconds later, Benicio strolled through the doors of Ethan's office in a polo shirt and chinos. Considering it was Thursday, he looked surprisingly casual, as if on vacation.

"I wasn't expecting you," Ethan said, getting to his feet.

"I took the day off to run errands—doctor appointment, that kind of thing. I was in the neighborhood and thought I'd stop by to say hi." Benicio sat in the burgundy guest chair.

Despite what his stepfather said, Ethan suspected a deeper reason for the visit. Whatever Benicio needed, he would oblige.

He didn't know what he would be doing right now if not for Benicio. Eighteen years ago, instead of buying him the car he wanted for graduation, his stepfather gave him the deed to a rundown property and loaned him the money to fix it up. He told him when he had flipped the house and made a profit, he could buy his own car.

That first house sparked his love of real estate and directed him on the path to becoming the first of the Connor-Santanas to become a billionaire.

"Can I get you something to drink?" Ethan asked, reclaiming his seat.

"No, no. Not necessary at all." Benicio waved away the suggestion. He smoothed his fingers along the armrest of the chair. "It is not completely true that I happened to be in the neighborhood," he said.

"What can I do for you, then?"

Their father-son relationship meant they could discuss almost anything, and if there was a problem, Ethan wanted to help.

"Not what you can do for me, but what I can do for you."

Both of Ethan's eyebrows lifted toward the ceiling.

"Do not be upset, but I talked to Bruno, and he told me about you and Skye."

Ethan muttered a low curse. He and Bruno talked a couple of days ago, and he mentioned the problems with Skye. "Bruno blabbed."

Benicio lifted one shoulder in an elegant shrug. "He is your brother, he cares about you, and we all love Skye. What is going on?"

Ethan rubbed his temple, seriously contemplating a trip to Vegas to strangle his brother.

"Nothing for you to concern yourself about."

"Well, obviously, there is a problem. According to Bruno, Skye wants to get married, and you insist you will never marry again."

"Skye and I can work out our problems without family interference."

"I am not interfering. I am here to give advice, based on my vast wealth of knowledge acquired after sixty-five years on this earth. You will learn from this old man, who has made many mistakes. Two divorces, *mijo*." He held up two fingers. "I have plenty to teach you. Now, you love Skye, yes?"

Ethan reluctantly resigned himself to a conversation he didn't want. "Of course."

"*Bueno.* Then you have to fix this problem before you lose her. She is a good woman."

"What do you suggest?" Ethan asked, deciding to humor him.

"You need to reconnect with her. Spend some quality time together."

"We see each other every day."

"No," Benicio said, shaking his head. "You must do something special, such as take her on a trip. When was the last time you took a vacation? A real one. Not a day or two."

Ethan honestly couldn't remember the last time he and Skye had taken more than a few days together. Along with his other business responsibilities, the Horizon project occupied much of his time. Because of work obligations over the past couple of years, vacations remained on the back burner.

Knowing he hit a nerve, Benicio raised an eyebrow. "Rosa

told me you have been working very hard the past two years. She is worried about you, concerned you work too hard."

"Mom wants grandchildren," Ethan said dryly, shifting around papers on his desk.

"That is not so bad, to have more grandchildren."

Ethan chuckled, shaking his head. "The two of you are something else."

"We are not getting any younger," Benicio said gravely.

Ethan sighed. "All right, so you think if I take Skye on a trip, that will solve our problems?"

"Maybe not all, but sometimes a woman needs reassurance she matters to you, and if you are not going to marry her, spend quality time with her. Show her that she is still important to you—worth your attention for more than a day or two at a time."

Ethan tapped his thumb on the chair's padded armrest. He, a man who prided himself on action, didn't know how to fix the situation with Skye. The light was gone from her eyes. She seemed... resigned to being with him, and the thought chafed.

Maybe his stepfather was right. He and Skye hadn't taken more than a few days off in a couple of years. Their last trip was to Italy, more than two years ago, and even then, he'd worked part of the vacation.

A change of scenery might be what they needed, but his schedule was so tight right now, he couldn't take more than a week off.

"I'm going to take your advice."

Benicio slapped his palms together. "Excellent. You will see I am right."

"I appreciate your concern."

Benicio cleared his throat. "There is something else I want to talk to you about. This is a little awkward for me, but... it's about your mother. Is she... seeing anyone?"

The question took Ethan by surprise, and he sat forward, resting his forearms on the desk. "Not that I know of," he said slowly. "Why?"

"I have been thinking about her a lot lately. Thinking about how maybe I could have worked harder to save our marriage. I wonder if we could... rekindle our relationship."

"Oh, really?"

Benicio smirked at the skepticism in his voice. "I know what you are thinking, but it's been three years, and Rosa might have a different mind now. We get along very well. In fact, we get along great. I'm not seeing anyone, so I was wondering if she is."

"Do you remember why you broke up in the first place?" Ethan asked.

"Of course." Benicio shifted irritably in the chair.

"Do you?"

His stepfather sighed heavily.

"As long as you won't step down from your position as head of your companies, you can forget about a relationship with my mother. You know she won't change her mind."

"Because she is as stubborn as a goddamn ox," Benicio grumbled.

"Benicio, listen, I know this is hard. But my mother told you what she wanted, and you didn't give it to her."

"What she wants, and what I want, are at odds."

"You promised to step down from the businesses at sixty but didn't. She gave you a two-year grace period, and you still didn't follow through. You left her no choice."

"She had a choice," the older man muttered.

"You're sixty-five years old. When are you going to slow down and enjoy the fruits of your labor? My mother wants to spend more time with you. Take trips together. Go to the beach. Go sailing. Visit some part of the world you haven't before. Essentially, doing what you told *me* to do with Skye."

"A trip once or twice a year is not enough for Rosa. She wants me to give up my work, which I love. Should I make myself miserable to make her happy?" Benicio pushed to his feet.

Looking up at him, Ethan asked, "Aren't you miserable now?"

Benicio's jaw tightened, and his chest puffed up, as if he were about to go into a rant. Then his chest deflated, and he sighed. "Your mother and I are better off as friends. We're old and both too stubborn to change. Don't be like us. *Adios.*"

Benicio walked out the door, a little less spring in his step than when he first arrived.

Ethan tapped his pen on the desk, ruminating on his stepfather's words.

His parents were probably still in love with each other, and as Benicio said, simply too stubborn to change.

He stopped tapping.

Stubborn, like him and Skye.

Chapter Eleven

"I'll be right back," Skye said.

She slipped away from the table where they were having dinner at Rico's.

They hadn't made love in over two weeks and barely touched in the same timeframe. Ethan's body burned for hers in an almost feral way. Yawning need raked his loins as he watched her wind through tables of diners in a silk blouse and black slacks that hugged her wide hips and put a spotlight on her great ass. He quietly suffered under the torment of his desire to make love to her, almost bending her over the breakfast table that very morning.

The emotional distance between them remained as wide as a chasm and affected him in an aggravating way. The past few nights he hadn't slept well, waking up once or twice, as if to confirm she was there and hadn't sneaked away in the dead of the night.

He wanted their life back to normal. He wanted her laughter at his sarcastic jokes and her whispered "*Stop*" right before she doubled over in laughter. He wanted her eyes glazed over and incessant whimpers as he plunged deep into her body while gripping her fleshy ass in both hands.

As she returned to the table, his eyes lingered on her shapely curves, and his body hardened with the need to slide into her and relieve the sexual frustration burning through his blood.

Benicio was right. They needed a change, a reset.

Skye sat down and took a sip of her after-dinner coffee, an accompaniment with the cheesecake on the plate in front of her.

"I have an idea," Ethan said.

She looked expectantly at him, slipping a piece of the cheesecake between her red lips. Perfectly innocent, yet a decadently sensual movement that reminded him of the way she'd take his dick in her mouth and make eye contact while she sucked him to a shuddering release.

Ethan stifled a groan and resettled in the chair. "Let's take a trip, go on a vacation."

Her eyebrows raised in surprise, and she swallowed—the same way she swallowed his come after she'd weakened him to the point of exploding.

"Why do you want to take a trip all of a sudden?" she asked.

He shrugged negligently. "We haven't taken a vacation in a while. Short trips here and there, but nothing longer than a few days. We should take a week and get away for a bit. I think it would be good for us."

She carefully placed her fork on the table. "I'm not sure I can get away."

"If I can, you can."

"Because my work isn't as important as yours?" she asked sweetly—too sweetly.

"Your work is important, but let's not be absurd and pretend I don't have more responsibilities than you do."

She gave a slight nod to indicate he had a point, for which he was relieved. He'd half expected her to start a fight.

"Okay, Ethan, if we do go on vacation, we need to take a real vacation. You can't be on the phone half the time. You have to cut off communication with your office and *relax*."

"Sweetheart, I run a multibillion-dollar company with offices around the world and thousands of employees. I'm in the middle of a sensitive deal in China, and although phase one of the Horizon development is nearing completion, problems crop up every couple of weeks. I can't go off the grid." Considering the conversation over, he took a sip of coffee.

"Yes, you can." Skye rested her arms on the table, her dark eyes steady as they locked with his. "At least, you should be able to. Otherwise, why do all of this? What's the point if you can't take a one-week break every now and again? So maybe you miss a phone call and lose a few thousand dollars. Maybe even a few million. So what? You have millions more and your whole company won't collapse. Wrap up your most important projects before we go, and leave the rest to your employees. If you did your job right, they should be able to survive a week without you. If they can't, then you either didn't hire the right people, or you didn't train them well. Either way, the fault is yours, and you need to get your shit together."

Quiet descended on the table, the only sound the buzz of conversations and utensils scraping the plates around them. Skye bit the corner of her mouth—as if she said too much—but didn't drop her gaze.

"How long have you been waiting to say that?" Ethan swallowed another mouthful of coffee.

She sat up straight and shrugged one shoulder. "A while."

Ethan

Ethan took her hand on the table and threaded their fingers together. Her fingers were so soft, like the rest of her body, and her nails painted a deep wine color.

"You're right. We should have time away without distractions."

"Really?" An immediate sparkle came into her eyes, and she perked up.

A twinge of guilt landed in Ethan's chest. Had he really been so ignorant of her desire for a business-free trip? Why hadn't she revealed her concerns before?

"Of course. If that's what you want."

"Where are we going to go?" she asked.

"You decide," Ethan said, feeling indulgent.

"Are you sure you want me to do that?" she asked playfully, and his heart rate ticked up a bit faster. For the first time in days, their relationship edged closer to normal.

"Pick a country you've always wanted to see, and that's where we'll go."

A smile of pleasure touched her lips, and the sight of her happiness warmed deep inside his chest. He would give her anything she asked for to keep that expression on her face—well, almost anything. For a millisecond, his gaze dropped to her left hand, fingers still intertwined with his. There had been no mention again of getting married or a ring, but the wall between them remained—as thin as rice paper, but a wall nonetheless.

"Let's go somewhere off the beaten path. No luxury hotels. Just a beach and warm weather," Skye suggested.

"Sounds like you already have a place in mind."

"Belize. When you went there on business a couple of years ago, you told me it was a beautiful country with friendly people, and how you wished you'd had more time to spend

71

there. I looked at travel sites to see about taking a trip at some point, but I stopped my research because you've been so busy the past couple of years."

"I would like to see more of the country than I did when I was there last. Belize it is, then. Get with Layla, and the two of you can plan the trip," Ethan said.

"And you'll wrap up all your major projects, so we can relax and have a real vacation?" she asked.

How bad had he been that she needed to insist?

"You have my word."

For the first time in weeks, the smile on her lips matched the smile in her eyes, and the lurking darkness disappeared. He lifted her palm to his mouth and watched her eyes darken with desire. Maybe tonight he'd experience those soft fingers on his skin and those red nails raking his back. If not tonight, very soon.

"I'll take care of everything," Skye whispered.

Whenever they traveled together, she and Layla handled the arrangements. Sometimes he contributed his thoughts, and other times they made the reservations without his input.

This time he'd let them do all the planning. This was his gift to her, to make up for the rift that had formed between them.

"How soon can you get away?" Skye asked.

"How about next week?"

"So soon?" Her eyebrows lifted in surprise, but her voice screamed delight.

"This trip is well overdue, and a few days is plenty of time for me to get my 'shit together' at work."

She laughed and tilted her head to the side, the look of adoration he craved making a comeback. The flesh between his legs became inflamed, hardening in anticipation.

"Thank you, baby," she said softly.

He kissed her hand again and looked forward to better days ahead.

His Skye was coming back to him.

Chapter Twelve

On the following Tuesday, Ethan and Skye flew first class from Atlanta to Belize City, a short three-hours-and-ten-minute direct flight.

They arrived at Goldson International Airport, and after they deplaned, walked along the tarmac to the terminal building with the rest of the passengers. Going through immigration and customs didn't take long, and soon they went outside, searching for their guide among the sea of brown faces holding up signs near the door.

"There he is," Skye said, pointing to a short, squat-looking man in a white polo shirt and khaki cargo shorts. He held a sign with their names on it.

The man's face broadened into a friendly smile. "Mr. Ethan? Miss Skye?"

"Just Ethan and Skye is fine," Ethan said, extending his hand.

"I'm Emil." He appeared to be in his late forties. "I'll be taking you to the house in Hopkins Village. Hopkins is located approximately two and a half hours from here. But the ride passes quickly, and there's plenty to see along the way." He spoke with an accent reminiscent of the islands in the Caribbean.

"We're looking forward to it," Ethan said.

"You needed a getaway, eh?"

"You could say that."

He glanced at Skye, who nodded her agreement, her expression hidden behind the large sunglasses over her eyes.

For the trip, she'd worn a floral print maxi-dress with short sleeves, the long hemline gently billowing around her ankles when she moved. The dominant rust color looked great against her tawny-gold skin, and the crossover bodice emphasized her magnificent breasts and repeatedly drew Ethan's eyes.

"There is no other place like Belize in the world. The perfect escape from your fast-paced life," Emil said.

Ethan and Skye each brought a suitcase and a carry-on bag, and Ethan helped Emil place their luggage in the back of the Jeep.

"Would you like to stop and get something to eat on your way to the house?" Emil asked.

Ethan looked at Skye, and she shook her head. "We can wait," he said.

"All right. Let's go."

Ethan and Skye climbed into the back of the Jeep, and soon they were on their way to the seaside village. Ethan didn't know much about the place, not having time to do much research as he wrapped up his work to keep his promise to Skye to be more present on their trip. He did know, however, that she and Layla chose a location less frequented by tourists, therefore less commercialized and crowded than other places in the country.

"Is this your first time here?" Emil asked, pulling out of the airport parking lot.

A colorful sign stretched across the road said *Welcome to Belize.*

Ethan answered. "It's the first time for Skye in Belize, but I've been here before, exploring real estate opportunities in Placencia and Ambergris Caye. I only stayed a few days and didn't have a chance to do any sightseeing."

"How long are you here this time?"

"One week."

"You can do a lot in a week. The local guides in Hopkins Village are very knowledgeable and can take you to spots for the best fishing and diving, if you like that kind of thing. You have to visit the Mayan ruins, of course, and you can't go wrong with Belizean food. When we pass through the town, I'll point out the best restaurant for eating local dishes like hudut, and the resorts near where you're staying have restaurants that serve delicious meals."

Emil pointed to a large structure to the right. "That's our prison. We only have one in the country."

"How many inmates?" Skye asked.

"About one thousand."

Emil talked most of the way, pointing out the entrance to the Belize Zoo and new developments, such as the road they traveled on, which connected the various villages and towns.

The hours sped by with him as their guide. He told them many of the houses were on stilts, explaining people built their homes that way to avoid floodwaters and allow for cooler air to circulate through their homes.

When they arrived in Hopkins Village, he drove slowly down the Main Street, a small community of shops and restaurants with the occasional guest lodging sprinkled in. They drove past a stand where a man sold bananas, potatoes, and other fruits and vegetables. A few kids chased each other across the street, and several motorbikes cruised past. Emil explained they were a popular mode of transportation because of the high gas prices.

He took them down a dirt road running parallel to the coast, toward the resorts. They bounced and jostled in the seats due to huge potholes, but he was kind enough to keep the vehicle at a slow pace. Despite the rough road, the buildings were in good shape.

"The Smoothie Café," Emil said, pointing. "A convenient place for snacks if you don't want a big meal. They have a really good bakery, their smoothies are tasty, and you can get freshly made sandwiches for lunch and breakfast in the morning. On the opposite side is the Iguana Resort. Let me tell you, they have the best oxtail tacos and a mango salsa..." He broke off, shaking his head as if the memory of the taste was so unbelievable he couldn't finish the sentence. "You can't leave without trying both."

"They must be really excellent," Skye said with some amusement.

Emil's eyes lifted to the rearview mirror. "Excellent is an understatement," he said.

Other options for dining out included a two-story restaurant promising delicious hamburgers, and a mauve-colored building with an outdoor patio served a worthwhile sit-down meal, according to Emil.

They pulled up outside of the white, one-story house Skye had rented, and Emil hopped out and opened the back door. At the same time, a young Black woman who looked to be in her mid-twenties exited the house and came down the front steps.

"Hello! I'm Bernice, the property manager." She extended a hand.

After introductions and pleasantries exchanged about the flight and drive from the airport, Bernice said, "Let me show you the house. Don't worry about your bags. Emil will take care of them for you." She led the way up the stairs.

The house was surrounded by banana trees and tall coconut trees, their broom-like leaves swaying in the refreshing tropical breeze. A winding white staircase led to the rooftop, where Bernice said they had a great view of the water, including some cays in the distance.

Upon entering the house, Ethan was pleasantly surprised. Skye used the word "rustic" when describing the property, and he'd wondered what the place would look like. While it wasn't luxurious, it was modern, clean, and comfortable-looking.

The house was small but contained two bedrooms and boasted an open floor plan with high ceilings. There was a living room and a kitchen with mahogany cabinets and new stainless steel appliances—a gas stove, microwave above the double sink, and a double-door refrigerator. A water cooler beside the refrigerator provided fresh water, and if they ran out, Bernice said they could call and within minutes she'd send someone with a new bottle. Ethan didn't anticipate them doing much cooking, but everything they needed were in the cabinets —utensils, plates, and pots and pans.

As Bernice showed them the first bedroom, she explained that the flooring throughout was made of cabbage-bark hard-wood. The master bedroom was about a third of the size of Ethan's dressing room but contained a king bed with a metal frame and French doors leading outside.

Their last stop was to the back veranda, where lounge chairs and a colorful striped hammock invited the home's occu-pants to relax. Only steps away, the warm waters of the Caribbean Sea lapped at the shore.

"Is everything to your liking?" Bernice asked.

"Perfect," Skye said, a satisfied smile on her lips. It was clearly the kind of getaway she'd wanted.

"Wonderful." Bernice beamed. "Here are your keys. Feel free to explore the area. There are resorts down the beach on either side. To your right is a beach bar. Vincent makes great pina coladas or anything else you'd like, from five in the afternoon until midnight. The beach is very safe, and this time of year, you won't see a lot of other guests. A good thing, because it means you'll mostly have the beach to yourself, and it will be easy to book tours and other leisure activities. If you need me, I'm a phone call away, or you can go to the bar and follow the signs to my office."

She left, and Ethan tipped Emil, thanking him for bringing in the bags and the interesting narrative on the trip there. He found Skye out the veranda, gazing out at the blue water.

"It's peaceful," she said. "I'll be happy here, but you're used to more luxurious accommodations."

"I'll survive," he said. "The house is nice, and the location away from the usual tourist traps was a good idea. Anyway, this trip isn't about me. It's about you. Us."

He couldn't see her eyes behind the sunglasses, but her lips fractionally tipped up in the corners.

She glided over to him and slid an arm around his waist. She tipped back her head, and he dropped a kiss to her puckered lips. "Thank you for being open-minded," she said.

She disappeared inside the house. Ethan didn't follow right away, listening to the waves wash up on the shore. He'd only been in the country a few hours but already felt himself relaxing. Maybe this trip wasn't only good for their relationship, but for him as well. He seldom took a vacation, and when he did, he worked much of the time, as Skye had pointed out.

A slower pace and sketchy Internet service might be what he needed for a better grasp on life and a chance to tone down the constant go-go mentality dominating his life.

He found Skye in the kitchen drinking water from a plastic cup.

"We should look into options for dinner," he said. "We could go next door or—"

Skye let out a squeal and hopped over to him. She grabbed his arm, and he saw what had caused her fright. A green lizard skittered across the floor.

"We have a guest," he said.

"Ethan, get rid of it. You know I don't like reptiles." She shivered and slid behind him.

Snakes, iguanas, and lizards all gave her the creeps.

"He's probably more afraid of you than you are of him."

"Whatever. Just *get rid of it*."

"Open the back the door," he instructed.

She did as he asked and backed away.

Taking the broom leaning against the wall, he cornered the lizard and swept it toward the open the door. The little creature appeared stunned for a moment, and Ethan took advantage and swept again, this time swooping it through the door.

As the lizard scampered away, Skye closed the door and breathed a sigh of relief. "I hope that's the last we see of him."

"Lizards are good to have around. They eat bugs."

"Bugs. Oh great."

He laughed at her, and she laughed too. Once again he was pleased to see a genuine smile on her face.

Chapter Thirteen

Skye took a nap while Ethan explored the area.

When she woke up, she was hungry and ready for dinner. Taking advice from Bernice, they decided on the Driftwood Beach Bar and Pizza Shack, a restaurant known for its jovial staff and located in town on the beach. Bernice called them a taxi, and the driver arrived in an older model, dusty black sedan—clearly a personal vehicle that had been dubbed a 'taxi.'

"Your chariot awaits," the man said with a sweep of his hand.

Skye appreciated his sense of humor, chuckling to herself when she saw Ethan's skeptical expression. So far Belizeans were a friendly bunch, and she was already making mental plans to return one day.

Because the village was so small, they arrived at their destination within minutes.

"You're in luck. The Garifuna drummers are playing tonight. Enjoy your meal!" the driver said.

Skye looked forward to the musicians because she'd read

about them in one of the pamphlets back at the house. Hopkins Village was the cultural center of the Garifuna people, descendants of Caribbean Indians and Africans from a shipwrecked slave ship who had intermarried and founded a new ethnic group and unique culture. Their history was filled with persecution and forced migration due to broken treaties with the British and the need to avoid enslavement, ending with settlements along the Central America coastline. Their dances, language, and food heavily influenced the culture of Hopkins Village.

The restaurant was right on the beach and consisted of a main building and several smaller buildings beside it that looked like residences. A sloping, thatched roof made of palm fronds added an authentic tropical twist. The main restaurant was open and mostly without walls, allowing air to flow from the front to the back.

The place was half-filled already, all the stools at the bar occupied with patrons, and the picnic-style tables in the dining area almost all occupied with couples and small families. As soon as they entered, a young woman greeted them and escorted them to one of the tables.

They crossed the slatted wood floor and sat next to a family of four. Ethan faced the door, and Skye sat opposite him with a view of the empty space where the musicians were likely to play later. After making sure to tell the waitress about his food allergy, they ordered two medium pizzas.

Ethan chose the Mediterranean, covered in artichokes, black olives, sun-dried tomatoes, roasted garlic, and feta cheese. Feeling adventurous, Skye ordered the barbecue chicken, topped with bacon, caramelized onions, and cilantro. They selected Belikin beer to drink, the country's locally brewed beer. Neither of them drank beer often, but they wanted the full Belizean experience.

Ethan

"You're in a good mood," Ethan remarked.

She was. The time away might have been exactly what she needed.

Skye combed her fingers through her sleek ponytail. "Maybe I am. I'm well-rested and plan to enjoy myself. How was your walk this afternoon?"

"I learned more about the area. Near Bernice's office, there's an Italian restaurant where we can have dinner one night, and a little convenience store where they sell snacks and toiletries. There's also a small tour office nearby with options for excursions, but we can also book at any of the resorts."

"What do you want to do?"

"As little as possible. This is supposed to be a relaxing vacation."

"Don't tell me you're actually enjoying the down time," Skye teased.

He chuckled. "I didn't like the idea of being cut off from my work, but I'm already settling into the idea."

"Where is your phone?"

"The business phone is back at the house. The personal phone is right here." He patted his pocket. "I haven't looked at my business phone for hours. I suggest we take it easy, but we do need to plan for the Mayan ruins. It's an all-day trip because the structures are a couple of hours away."

Skye rested her chin on her palm. "I like the idea of taking it easy, hanging out at the beach or on the veranda."

"In a bikini," Ethan added, dropping his voice.

"Yes, in my bikini." She blushed. "I wasn't sure at first, but I'm glad we took this trip."

Ethan nodded slowly. "I know. I had the distinct feeling you weren't happy. For all I knew, you were planning to suffocate me while I slept."

She giggled. "If I wanted to kill you, there's a much easier

83

way. I could do that at any time by slipping shrimp in one of your meals and conveniently leaving your EpiPen at home."

Ethan stared at her in silence.

The smile fell off her lips. "I'm kidding."

The beers arrived. "Your pizzas will be ready in a few minutes," the waitress promised before walking away.

The atmosphere at the table took on a heavy quality.

"I'm sorry, I shouldn't have made such a horrible joke," Skye said.

Ethan sampled the beer. "It's good." He carefully placed the bottle on the table. "I'm pretty sure Joanne used to do that."

Skye froze and drew in a sharp breath. "What?"

"She was a real bitch." Ethan took another swig, a longer drag this time, as if he needed it. "During our marriage, there were a number of incidences where, somehow, shellfish got in my food. Not a lot of times, but often enough that it was *unusual*. I became hypervigilant about everything I ate and sometimes wouldn't eat at the house. I'd have dinner out and then go home, and if we ate at a new restaurant, I made sure I talked to the manager multiple times to avoid mistakes. I became... paranoid, for lack of a better word. She never admitted to doing it, but I'm certain that she did. I think she liked watching me suffer. Liked having power over me."

"That's quite an accusation."

"I've only had one major incident in the eleven years since we've been divorced."

Skye had seen him have allergic reactions a handful of times, but they were minor. "What did you see in her?"

A bitter smile crossed his lips. "My mother and Benicio, they warned me, but I was young and confused lust with love and ignored the red flags until too late. Didn't listen to any of their advice or warnings. By the time I realized my mistake, I was determined to make our marriage work. Not only because we were married, but to prove them wrong."

"You're so stubborn. She could have killed you." Her voice shook.

All of a sudden, Skye hated Joanne with a passion. Hated her for hurting Ethan and causing him to distrust. Because of her, he kept Skye at arm's length. If she ever saw that bitch in person she might punch her in the face.

"I would never do something like that to you," Skye said.

"I know."

She tasted her beer, enjoying the richness of the flavor, and then replaced the bottle on the table's wood surface. "Do you see red flags in me?" she asked in a small voice. Maybe the hesitation to marry her didn't have anything to do with Joanne. Maybe something he saw made him think twice about marrying her.

"No."

A simple answer, yet she wondered if he were being completely honest.

The pizzas arrived, and they exchanged slices to try each other's pie. The conversation moved to other topics, but Skye marveled at how, after all this time, Ethan had finally opened up about the most forbidden topic in their relationship. The fact that he had shared something so personal made Skye feel closer to him in a way she hadn't in a while.

They were almost finished with their meal when the eight members of the Garifuna band arrived with their instruments, set up, and started their performance. The six men, who included two singers, three drummers, and a man shaking a shakka—or maracas—wore colorful dashiki-style shirts over jeans or long shorts. The two women in the group wore traditional long dresses and colorful head wraps and danced to the music the men beat out on the drums.

Delaney Diamond

Skye swayed to the music and caught the eye of one of the women. She signaled for Skye to join them, but Skye shook her head. Undeterred, the young woman danced over, hips swaying from side to side, and gently pulled Skye to her feet. The audience cheered and applauded encouragingly, including Ethan.

At first she was embarrassed, but then Skye gave herself over to the beat of the drums and followed the hip movements of the younger women. She tuned out the patrons and employees and simply enjoyed herself, a couple of times making eye contact with Ethan and casting flirtatious looks in his direction. A faint smile touched his lips, but blatant hunger filled his eyes as they followed the swing of her gyrating hips.

At the end of the song, the entire restaurant erupted into loud applause. Laughing, Skye thanked the women and moved to go back to her seat, but Ethan grabbed her hand and pulled her down on the bench beside him. His hungry kiss devoured her lips, and she leaned into the passion with equal fervor.

When they withdrew, she relaxed as he slipped an arm across her shoulders, and they spent the rest of the evening watching the performance with her close at his side.

Chapter Fourteen

Skye stretched and yawned on her lounge chair, utterly content with her current situation. The soothing sounds of the water kissing the shoreline had lulled her into a brief nap.

Her eyes focused on Ethan, who was walking out of the sea, water dripping off his mahogany-brown skin. The sun glistened and danced on the muscles carved into his body. He was magnificent in a pair of dark green trunks—firm biceps, thick muscular thighs, and strong-looking calves.

Her loins stirred with desire, which remained unsatisfied after last night.

She and Ethan left the restaurant very late. Sitting close to him for the rest of the night had aroused her, and she'd fully expected to make love when they arrived at the house. Instead, they both climbed into bed, and he simply pulled her close and said good night.

She had been perplexed, even disappointed, but this morning she realized that had been the right decision. They had both been exhausted because she had no recollection of what happened after her head hit the pillow. It seemed only seconds had passed until she woke up in bed alone.

She had found Ethan in the kitchen, having not too long before returned from picking up breakfast from one of the nearby resorts. He was a morning person—getting up at a godawful hour every morning to check the financial news and eat breakfast. She, on the other hand, preferred to lounge in bed for as long as possible and was known to hit the snooze two —or five—times each morning.

Ethan brought eggs, ham, bacon, fruit, and several types of bread packed neatly in boxes. They made coffee and sat on the veranda, enjoying the morning breeze as they ate breakfast.

Afterward, she put on her orange halter-top bikini—one of Ethan's favorites—and they went swimming. They spent the morning alternating between swimming in the warm waters, walking back and forth along the beach, and relaxing in the chairs they moved from the veranda onto the sand beneath the shade of the coconut trees.

"What do you want to do for lunch?" Ethan asked, lifting his towel from the chair beside her and drying his skin.

"How about we go to that one resort and try those famous oxtail tacos Emil raved about."

"The Iguana Resort," Ethan supplied. "Don't forget, we have to try the mango salsa too."

"How could I? I think he had a spiritual experience when he talked about them," she laughed.

"They better be as good as he says they are," Ethan said.

Skye giggled, reluctantly rising from the chair. Despite not wanting to leave her comfortable spot, she was hungry. "I need to take a shower and wash my hair, and then we can go," she said, following Ethan into the house. "Let's tour the town tomorrow and try the restaurant with the hudut, and on Friday or Saturday we can go to the Mayan ruins. I was reading about their history and definitely want to see them before we go home. I won't be long," she said, heading into the bedroom.

Skye undressed and went into the bathroom. There was no shower curtain or door, only a beveled half wall to contain the spray. She stepped onto the cool tile and reach up to turn on the water, only to find a pair of tiny eyes looking at her from several feet above. The green lizard was back.

She screamed and hopped out of the shower.

Seconds later, Ethan burst through the door.

"He's back." Skye pointed at the stall.

Ethan peered in. "There's nothing to be afraid of. I told you before, he's probably more afraid of you than you are of him."

"I seriously doubt that since he keeps coming up in here, in *our* space."

"He's not going to bite you."

"No, but he could jump on top of me while I'm taking a shower." She shivered in disgust. "Get rid of it, Ethan."

His eyes dropped to her breasts. "If you like, I can stay in here and protect you."

She'd forgotten she was stark naked. "Not funny." She snatched up a towel and held it in front of her.

"I thought it was," he muttered.

"Would you please get him out of here?"

"If I try to catch him, he'll probably run higher up the wall. I'll have to be strategic."

"I'll let you figure that out." Skye hurried from the room.

She sat on the arm of one of the chairs in the living room, and Ethan came out and took the broom, a bowl, and a plate into the bathroom.

"What are you doing with all of those?" Skye called.

"Let me worry about that. You stay your pretty little behind out here and let me handle this."

"Yes, sir."

After a minute or two, Ethan exited the bathroom with the plate over the bowl.

"Eww. Is he in there?" Skye whispered.

"Yes. Do you want to see him?"

She hopped up from the chair. "No! Get it out of here. Maybe you should kill him so he doesn't come back."

Ethan shot her a glance.

"Fine, don't kill him, but he better not show his face around here again."

Ethan released the lizard to the outside, dumped the dishes in the sink, and washed his hands.

Skye sidled over and wrapped her arms around his waist. "My hero," she murmured, kissing his back and running her hands up and down his naked chest.

"You know you can't rub on me and expect me to stand here and do nothing." He turned to face her.

"We were both at the beach. We should both take a shower," Skye suggested with false innocence.

"Hm. You make a good point."

She took his hand and led the way into the bathroom. She removed the towel and then helped Ethan out of his swim trunks.

They climbed into the shower together and let the water run over their skin. Ethan made sure to brush off the sand, paying extra attention to her breasts and ass. Her skin tingled with every stroke, and she returned the favor by running her hands over his muscular body, indulging the need for further contact by kissing his chest, licking his nipples, and nipping at his Adam's apple.

Ethan squeezed moisturizing shampoo in his hands and proceeded to wash her hair. Instead of standing behind her, he stood in front, and she wrapped her arms around his torso. They were skin to skin as he worked his magic.

She always enjoyed when he washed her hair, which was nothing like going to the salon. Ethan's hands were gentle but firm as he massaged the lather through the strands. The scent of the shampoo's herbal oils filled her nostrils and added to the sensual experience of him taking his time to give her the simple pleasure.

Skye closed her eyes and tipped back her head, humming her pleasure as his fingertips moved along her temple to the base of her skull. Ethan followed with the deep penetrating conditioner, and in between the washing and conditioning, his lips found their way onto her shoulders, and every so often his hands splayed across her rib cage and squeezed her breasts.

By the time he finished, she was a quivering mass of raw nerves, ready to straddle his hips and ride him to oblivion.

They left the shower and Skye wrapped a towel around her hair while Ethan took his time rubbing her dry with the soft towel. When he finished, her nipples were hard and a crimson blush stained her cheeks.

"Ethan," she breathed, sliding an arm around his neck.

That was all he needed to hear.

His lips locked over hers, and his hands gripped her ass, lifting her core against his hard length in a rapid walk to the bedroom.

Chapter Fifteen

S kye was already wet, and not from the shower. Her body was so attuned to Ethan's that his kisses alone had her hungering for his possession. As they lowered onto the bed, their arms and legs tangled together in the soft sheets, and her sex pulsed, a fist of need tightening in the base of her abdomen.

Ethan fastened his lips to hers and darted his tongue into her mouth, and she became intoxicated by the thrill of his taste. Sandwiched between him and the bed, she locked her arms behind his neck to bind him close so she could indulge her senses and satisfy the craving for him.

Aching to make up for the long days she was deprived of his touch, she sucked his tongue with wanton aggression and grinded her hips into his, her lustful movements wrenching a masculine groan from the deepness of his chest. His hands on her rib cage swept the curve of her waist and hips as he buried his head between her breasts and released a grumble of satisfaction.

Ethan toyed mercilessly with her breasts. He knew they

were sensitive and paid them extra attention. Cupping the lush mounds, he planted hot kisses all over them. While he sucked one nipple, his thumb played with the other. All she could do was whimper and bow her back in response, gasping as the abrasive edge of his teeth and the suction of his mouth wreaked havoc on the sensitive tips.

Sliding down her body, he kissed everywhere, and Skye watched him go lower, almost beside herself as he pried her legs apart, his mouth seeking her aroused flesh.

"I missed kissing you here."

He lowered his face between her thighs and her fingers clutched his shoulders at first contact. The kiss was soft and gentle in pressure, and Skye writhed in frustration when he didn't repeat it.

"Missed licking you here."

He licked her slowly, the lazy stroke of his tongue causing her toes to curl and her fingers to fasten tighter around the back of his head.

"Ethan," she breathed, tossing her head from one side to the next until the towel on her head broke free.

Ethan notched his mouth to her aching sex and gave her engorged clit the abundance of his focus. He lapped at her arousal with the type of relish typical of a man dining on the tastiest of meals. Each smack of his lips and groan in his throat added to the chorus of lewd sounds filling the bedroom. He tortured her plumped flesh, alternating the use of his tongue and teeth to draw gasping, agonized cries from her lips.

Skye never tired of the sensation of his mouth on the most intimate part of her body, and Ethan remained merciless in his undivided attention. In the heat of their passion, she undulated her hips as the tightening in her loins rose to a crescendo and pushed her toward the edge.

"Baby..." Skye whimpered.

She barely got the word out when a deluge of sensation crashed into her loins, and her feverish body exploded into a convulsive chain of spasms.

Ethan lifted from between her legs, and Skye grieved the loss of contact. Gasping in completion, she closed her eyes, lips parted and back arched as the pleasure didn't relent and swallowed her whole. Every part of her buzzed with sensation—her nipples and breasts, her hips and thighs, her belly and calves and toes and hands. Nowhere remained untouched by the fantastic orgasm she just experienced.

Ethan raised onto his knees, and she caught her breath in admiration of his incredibly fine body. He exuded strength, from the top of his broad shoulders to the jutting erection she anxiously awaited to claim her.

He dragged his hands down her calves and lifted one foot to his mouth. He kissed her toes and the bottom of her foot and then moved across her ankle up to the calf. His electrifying touch made the inside of her thighs quiver, and each time his mouth connected to her hypersensitive skin, her body jerked a little from the enjoyment of it.

He did the same to her other leg, taking long moments to kiss and caress. Despite the splendid orgasm she experienced moments ago, by the time he finished, desire had risen in her again.

Bracing over Skye, Ethan looked down into her eyes. "Are you ready for me, sweetheart?"

"Yes."

There was no other answer to give.

Ethan nested between her thighs, and her knees clamped either side of his naked hips. Her palms coasted up his back, reveling in the hard muscles under his skin. She tilted her head up to kiss his throat and dragged her tongue along the line of his jaw.

As he penetrated her with his thick length, his mouth simultaneously crashed into hers and their harsh breaths collided. Skye's eager kisses were broken up by her heavy, panting moans. He felt so good, plunging deep, every now and again his coarse chest hairs grating against her tender nipples.

She rocked into his rhythm, one hand clawing the bedsheets, the other clutching his shoulder in a hard grip.

"You're so damn beautiful. You're everything to me, Skye. Don't ever doubt that. Everything."

Masculine grunts of pleasure were interwoven between the words of praise. And the words—they caused emotion to clog in her throat.

Her every thought was of Ethan. Not only as a lover but as the man of her dreams. He owned her, their lives so wrapped up in each other she didn't know where his ended and hers began.

His kisses set her blood aflame, and he consumed her with each demanding thrust. He was the love of her life. Her beginning, her end, her everything.

"Go deeper, baby, please," she begged.

Ethan lifted one leg over his arm and angled her hips higher. Then he shoved in deeper, and a violent shudder juddered through her body.

"I love you," Skye gasped.

After those words, she splintered into a thousand pieces, tumbling headlong into a blinding climax and pulsating around him, her passion-filled cries drowning out the sounds of his own wrenching release.

Afterward, Ethan placed gentle kisses from one side of her collarbone to the other. He kissed her cheeks and the tops of her breasts. It was as if he couldn't stop kissing her.

Eyes closed, Skye savored the affection, unable to move

even though the damp towel had twisted into a rope that rested in an uncomfortable position beneath her spine.

Ethan's weight remained on top of her, and Skye lazily ran her hands up and down his back. She inhaled the combined scent of his freshly showered skin and their lovemaking.

She wished to never lose this feeling—this feeling of complete and utter contentment with the man she loved.

Chapter Sixteen

For lunch on Thursday, Skye and Thresa took a leisurely stroll to The Greasy Spoon, a small restaurant down the street from the Decatur Student Learning Center, and chose a table near the window where they could look out at the side street. They didn't eat there often because the food wasn't exactly healthy, hence the name, but it was absolutely delicious. Juicy burgers, thick steak fries, and grilled hot dogs covered in caramelized onions were among the specialties.

They both ordered bacon cheeseburgers, fries, and large Cokes.

While they waited for the food to arrive, Thresa stretched her hands across the table and said, "Give it to me!"

Skye laughed and handed her friend the box she brought from the office. She and Ethan returned stateside yesterday morning, and she spent the afternoon first wrapping, then mailing off souvenirs. A few gifts could be hand delivered, and this was one of them. Wrapped in silver paper, a red bow on top, the box contained souvenirs for Thresa, but Skye refused to let her open it before now.

"There you go. I hope you love your gift."

"I'm sure I will." Thresa tore into the paper and then stopped. "You know you didn't have to do this, right?"

"I know, but I wanted to. Now open the darn box before I do!"

Thresa burst out laughing. Skye danced in the chair, barely able to contain her excitement as she watched her friend tearing off the wrapping.

Thresa gasped when she lifted out the treasure inside.

"It's a Mayan basket," Skye explained. "The Mayan women in southern Belize still do traditional basket weaving."

The basket, six inches high and eight inches wide with a lid, included a design woven into the fabric.

"I love it," Thresa said.

She removed the lid and pulled out the rolled up T-shirt Skye placed inside. On the front of the shirt was a beach scene and the words *You better Belize it!*

They both laughed.

"I can't wait to wear this," Thresa said, holding up the shirt and inspecting the front and back.

She carefully replaced the souvenirs and set the box on the floor beside the table. "Thank you for thinking of me. Now tell me everything. What happened, what did you see, what did you do?"

"It was a great experience. The house in the perfect spot, right on the beach and in between several resorts, so we visited them for meals a few times and rented a golf cart to go into the little village. The people are friendly, and the food we ate was outstanding. There's this dish called hudut—it's fish cooked in coconut milk and served with mashed plantains. Simple but tasty."

Skye went into further details, talking about the Garifuna people and their history, as well as talking about the visit she and Ethan took to the Mayan ruins.

She pulled out her phone and showed Thresa the photos. "That's us at the ruins of Xunantunich, a couple of hours drive from Hopkins Village."

Both she and Ethan were wearing sunglasses with an arm around each other. Ethan had refused to smile, as usual, but she was grinning from ear to ear. They took a couple of selfies, but the guide also took pictures for them. "That's a shot of Guatemala in the distance. We could see it from the top of the ruins."

"Wow. The two of you look like you had a great time. I'm so jealous," Thresa said, swiping through the photos on Skye's phone.

"I'm jealous of you," Skye said softly.

"Why? Because I stayed behind and worked while you soaked up the sun on a warm beach in Central America?" Thresa handed back the phone.

Skye knew she was teasing but couldn't quite get a smile on her face. "I never told you this, but Ethan and I were going through a rocky patch."

Thresa's eyes widened. "I had no idea."

Skye nodded. "It's complicated. To be honest, I'm not sure our relationship has completely healed, but I had a great time on the trip, and he's trying... to make me happy, you know?"

"What's wrong, if you don't mind my asking?"

The waitress arrived with their food and set down plates with the large burgers and fries. After making sure they had everything they needed, she moved on to the next table.

Skye dipped a fry in ketchup as she considered how to explain. "Ethan and I have been together for a long time, and the night of his brother's graduation party, we argued. I almost feel silly saying this right now, but I asked him about marriage, and he let me know marriage wasn't in the cards for us."

"That's tough." Thresa sipped her Coke, never taking her eyes from Skye.

"It was *very* tough to hear. He's anti-marriage because his first marriage ended in divorce, and his ex-wife was a piece of work. On the trip, he shared something with me that I still can't believe. He's called her a devil before, and now I understand why."

"Has his opinion about marriage changed since the trip?"

Skye shook her head, almost embarrassed to admit nothing had changed. "I can't force him to marry me."

"No, you can't." Thresa's eyebrows came together in a frown.

Skye wanted to remove the look of concern from her friend's face.

"He's good to me, and I know he loves me, so maybe that will have to be enough." She hated second-guessing herself.

"But if you're not happy..."

"I'm happy... most of the time. No relationship is perfect, right?"

"True," Thresa said, sounding unconvinced.

"Change of topic. We need to finalize plans for the play next Thursday."

They discussed changes to the set and the excitement the kids were feeling as the event drew near. The change in conversation kept Skye's mind clear of Ethan for a little while, which worked well. By the end of the meal, her spirits had lifted.

Thresa placed her money in the middle of the table, next to Skye's. "I'm going to run to the restroom before we go back to the center," she said.

She left the table, and while Skye drained the last of her

Coke from the glass, Trey, the owner and manager of The Greasy Spoon, approached.

"How was the burger?" He was taller than Ethan but lanky with a low-cut fade.

"Delicious as always, but I can't come in here too often." Skye laughed.

His eyes softened. "I don't think you have anything to worry about."

Trey always paid her compliments and flirted.

"Thank you," Skye said politely.

He sat across from her. "I heard the kids at the center are putting on play."

"Yes, next Thursday night. You should come, and donations are welcomed. Hint, hint."

He laughed.

"No, seriously, it's nice to receive support from the community," Skye said.

"I'll definitely be there and make attendance a requirement of the job for my staff. Anyone who doesn't attend the play is getting fired."

"Excellent."

They both laughed then.

"Well, I guess I'll leave you alone and get back to work. These burgers don't cook themselves."

"Nice talking to you."

Trey stood and started walking away, but then he made a one-eighty turn and came back to the table.

"I'm probably wasting my time, but I'm going to shoot my shot anyway. Would you like to get together sometime? Something simple like coffee, or I could cook you a delicious meal— much better than what you eat here, by the way."

"Oh... I... I can't."

"Let me guess. You're in a relationship. Of course you are.

Look at you." He bit his bottom lip, eyes skimming her upper body visible above the tabletop.

Skye laughed and subconsciously rubbed the back of her neck. "Yes, I am."

"Gotta admit I'm disappointed, but I'm still coming to the play. What time is it?"

"Seven o'clock," Skye answered.

"I'll leave here early and come by."

"That would be nice. Thank you."

"Sure. Anything for the kids." He flashed a grin.

Thresa approached the table.

"Ladies, you have a good afternoon," Trey said before walking away.

Skye stood, feeling her friend's eyes on her.

"What was that about?" Thresa asked, lifting her box from the floor.

"Who said that was about anything?" Skye asked, leading the way through the crowded dining room.

"Because he's always had a crush on you, which is obvious, and it seems he took advantage of my disappearance from the table."

They stepped into the bright day, and Skye slipped sunglasses over her eyes to shield them from the sun's rays. They started the short walk back to the learning center.

"I invited him to the play, and he said he'll come. But he also kinda asked me out."

"Ooh, sookie, sookie now. Ethan has some competition." Thresa did a shoulder shimmy.

Skye laughed and shoved her friend. "No, he doesn't. I explained to Trey that I'm in a relationship. Even if I weren't, Ethan and I have been together so long, I'm not sure I'd know how to act. Dating seems like a daunting task."

Relationships could be exhausting. So many moving parts,

such as the getting-to-know-you stage, the stage where you figure out if you like the person or not, and how to behave so they would like you, with all your quirks and oddities.

"Well, if things don't work out with Ethan, Trey seems like a nice guy. It doesn't hurt to know you have options."

"No it doesn't, does it?"

Chapter Seventeen

than's conference call was not going well. His liaison in China wanted him to fly to Beijing to smooth talks with the Chinese investors—a trip he definitely didn't want to take. Rushing off to China could jeopardize the small strides he'd made with Skye.

Since the trip to Belize a week ago, their relationship was in a better place, but he held no illusions that they were completely back to normal. An emotion he couldn't face lurked behind the veneer of her laughter and smiles. He questioned whether mentally she had truly forgiven him and accepted their relationship could not move beyond its current status.

Suzanne's crisp British voice came through the speakers. "If you fly out today, you can be here by the weekend, and we can work on strategy for Monday morning."

"I have an event to attend tonight that I can't get out of. I made a promise, but I can leave right after—around ten or so."

"That still gets you here by the weekend, but we'll have less time. Expect to be here for at least five days. Maybe as much as seven."

"I hope it won't take that long," Ethan muttered.

A message from Daria popped up in the chat box on his computer. *Your 2 o'clock appointment is here.*

"If I fly over there, I want to meet with the entire team. Not just a few of them, like last time," Ethan said, typing out a response. *Put them in the large conference room.*

"I can arrange for everyone to attend the meetings. So you'll be here by the weekend?"

He rubbed his temple, wishing he could say no. "Yes. I'll have my executive assistant make the arrangements and email the details to you."

"I'm terribly sorry about this Ethan, but it can't be helped. I'm sure once you get here we'll be able to sort this all out."

"We better. Thank you for the update, and I'll see you soon."

* * *

The only way to describe the energy backstage at the center's first theatrical production was nervous excitement times one hundred.

Skye desperately wanted the show to be a success for the kids. They had worked so hard for weeks. At the moment, she, Thresa, and two volunteers fixed costumes, calmed fears, and made last-minute adjustments to the set.

The play was an original about a baby dinosaur who became separated from her family during a snow storm. She set out to find her family, and during the trek met a wooly mammoth, a saber-toothed tiger, and other prehistoric animals who joined in the journey to reunite her with her family.

"Miss Thorpe?"

Skye paused in the middle of attaching wings to one of the

pterodactyls. A very nervous-looking eight-year-old bear stared up at her.

"I don't think I can do it," the little girl whispered.

"Sure you can. One minute."

Skye quickly finished attaching the Velcro wing to the little boy.

"Thank you, Miss Thorpe!" He ran off.

Skye dropped to her haunches in front of the girl. "What's wrong?"

"I'm scared. What if I forget my lines? Everybody will laugh at me." She sounded so distraught, her eyes wide with worry.

"Oh, honey, you're going to do just fine. Remember, we practiced and practiced. Why don't you tell me your lines now and let's see if you can remember them. What do you say when Diane Dinosaur starts going in the wrong direction?" After weeks of practice she knew the dialogue by heart.

The little girl took a deep breath. "Not that way, it's dangerous."

"Perfect. Good job! And what do you say when she asks, 'Where should I go, Betty Bear?'"

"Follow me. I'll show you the way."

Skye grinned. "See, you got it. That was excellent!"

The little girl grinned back. "I got it."

"You sure did. High five." Skye held up her palm and received a slap from the bear paw. "And don't forget, me and Miss Davis and the teachers will be right here. If you need help, all you have to do is look at us, and we'll help you. Okay?"

"Okay." With her confidence restored, the little bear scampered away.

"Is she okay?" Thresa asked.

Skye straightened to her full height. "A little bit of stage fright, but I think she'll be fine." She glanced at her watch. "We have ten minutes until the curtain rises. I'll—"

"Skye, Thresa!" Janelle rushed over to them.

The younger woman was in her late twenties, hair and makeup looking downright perfect—as usual—as if always on her way to a photo shoot.

Skye bristled. "Janelle, where have you been? It's almost show time," she said, unable to keep the irritation out of her voice.

Janelle called in to work that morning, and tonight they could have used her help preparing for the show.

"I know, I know, I'm so sorry. I'm still recovering from yesterday." She sighed dramatically.

"What happened yesterday?" Thresa asked.

"*This.*" Janelle stuck out her hand to show off a rock the size of Gibraltar attached to a platinum band. "I'm engaged!"

Both Thresa and Skye's mouth's fell open.

"You've only been dating six months," Thresa said.

"I know! He said when a man knows, he knows, and he didn't want to risk losing me. So he put a ring on it, honey!" She tossed her head and let her silky hair fly over her shoulder. "To be honest, I was expecting the proposal because he's been acting kind of suspicious. I thought he would propose last month, that's why I called in that Wednesday—do you remember?—but he didn't, and I was so bummed.

"Then yesterday he told me we were going out to dinner and said I should dress up. He took me to the Sun Dial *in the middle of the week,* so I knew something was up. I put on my baddest dress, which made my tits and ass look fantastic, and after dessert, he went down on one knee and popped the question!" Janelle squealed and ran in place. "Oh my goodness, we couldn't get out of bed all day today. Of course I had to call my family and friends. Then he and I talked, laughed, admired my ring, and made plans. I thought about missing tonight, but I had to tell you my good news."

Not because she wanted to be here for the kids and do her darn job. Nope, she wanted to brag about getting engaged. Skye silently fumed.

"Congratulations," she said flatly. "We should start rounding up the kids and getting them ready for when the curtain rises. Thresa's going to open with an explanation about the play, thank the parents, et cetera, et cetera, like we planned."

Janelle's smile tightened, and she splayed her fingers on her chest in a display of sympathy, making sure to use her left hand though she was right-handed. The ring sparkled under the stage lights.

"Oh, I'm sorry, Skye. How rude of me. I've been going on and on about my engagement, and here you are still single, after years of being with the same man. I can be so insensitive sometimes. Don't you worry, girl, I'm sure it'll happen for you soon. I'm gonna go put down my bag and get to work."

Skye's cheeks burned with embarrassment and anger. As Janelle sashayed away from them, Skye lunged for her, but Thresa grabbed her arms and held her back.

"She's not worth it," her friend said in a low voice.

"Did you hear what she said?"

"Yes, I did. Forget her. We have a production to put on."

"I'm gonna strangle her one of these days, I swear."

"And I'll help you hide the body, but tonight, we need to focus on the children. Take a breath. Woosah." Thresa demonstrated by breathing in deeply and then letting the air slowly release through her lips.

Skye closed her eyes and breathed in and out slowly. "Woosah."

"Perfect. Just ignore her." Thresa patted her arm.

Skye couldn't ignore the comment. Janelle sparked such anger because her words hit too close to home. She peered between the curtains at the crowd filing in. Since the recreation room doubled as their theater, the video games, ping-pong tables, tumbling mats, and other items had been removed or shoved to the outer edges of the space. Volunteers set up seventy-five folding chairs to accommodate the guests.

Unfortunately, some of the parents couldn't attend the production because they needed to work two or three jobs to make ends meet. Skye hired a videographer and photographer out of her own pocket to capture the production. Free copies of the video would be provided to any parent who wanted one, and she'd add the photos to the center's scrapbook.

Skye caught her breath when Ethan came down the center aisle in one of his three-piece suits, obviously having left work to come directly there. He looked distinguished and completely overdressed among the rest of the attendees. Several people looked curiously at him as he took a seat at the end of one row. Especially the women. One woman nudged her girlfriend, and they outright ogled him. Most days she ignored the blatant way the opposite sex made eyes at her man, but in light of Janelle's cutting comment, their reaction infuriated her.

Skye let the curtain fall back in place and promised herself she wouldn't allow Janelle's nasty comment to affect the evening. She had work to do.

Positive thoughts and a silent pep talk didn't quite do the trick, however. Because a dull ache remained in the center of her chest for the rest of the night.

Chapter Eighteen

After the show, proud parents and grinning, excited children surrounded Skye and her co-workers. Amazingly, only a few mishaps occurred among the actors and one set incident occurred when an "iceberg" near the back collapsed, causing Skye to ease onto the stage and set it upright again.

She lavished praise on the kids to their parents, joining them in eating sugar cookies and drinking the syrupy sweet punch. Then she and Thresa spent almost ten minutes answering a local reporter's questions about the performance and the work they did at the learning center.

Ethan helped the volunteers fold chairs and stack them in a back room, while Trey hovered nearby holding the hand of a little girl about eight years old, her hair styled in Fulani braids with beads at the end. Taking advantage of a free moment, Skye went to speak to them.

"You came," she said to Trey.

He grinned. "You doubted me? I wasn't just talking when I said I would come. Sadly, I couldn't convince any of my staff to join me, but it's probably for the best. Someone needs to stay behind and run the restaurant."

Skye laughed. "In that case, I forgive you. So, who is this lovely little girl?"

He placed a hand on the child's shoulder. "My daughter, Jasmine. Jasmine, say hello to Miss Thorpe."

"Hello, Miss Thorpe." They shook hands.

"Hello, Jasmine, nice to meet you. Did you two enjoy the play?" Skye asked Trey.

"I did!" Jasmine piped up.

Trey nodded. "I did too. Very funny, and those kids are hella talented. I know for a fact young Trey didn't have as much talent or courage to do what they did. Their parents much be proud. You and the staff have got to be patting yourselves on the back for a job well done."

"That's nice of you to say. Overall, we're definitely pleased with the results. Considering this was our first play, I think we did well." The staff and kids were already talking about doing another play.

"Daddy, can I have some punch and cookies?" Jasmine asked.

"Sure, go ahead."

His daughter ran to the table where one of the volunteers handed refreshments to guests.

"She's adorable," Skye said.

"Yeah, she is. That's my heart." Trey stuffed his hands in the pocket of his jeans. "I've never asked, but do you have kids of your own?"

"No, I don't."

Her gaze skipped to Ethan, and her breath hitched. He crouched in front of a little boy who sat on the floor—the pterodactyl from the play—giving guidance as the boy tied his shoelaces. Her chest tightened with longing. She'd seen Ethan with his nieces and nephew. Firm when needed, gentle in crucial moments—playful, protective, and loving. He would make an amazing father.

"Me and her mom divorced three years ago," Trey said. "The split was tough at first, not being able to see Jasmine every day. All the things that used to annoy me—her loud screaming through the house, climbing in our bed on Saturday morning and waking us up with her stinky morning breath—I missed all that shit. Me and her mom struggled for balance the first year or so, but now we're in a good place." His gaze rested lovingly on his daughter in a small circle of kids—talking, munching on cookies, and drinking punch.

"So you worked out your differences for her sake," Skye said.

"Definitely."

"Think you'll ever marry again?"

His gaze shifted back to her. "Yeah, I'd like to. I'm hoping an opportunity opens up for me real soon." The way he looked at her suggested *she* was the opportunity he waited on.

Skye smiled uneasily, rubbing a hand along the side of her neck. "I wish you luck with that."

Hands deep in his pockets, he leaned closer and dropped his voice. "You know I'm talking about you, right?"

Skye eased back. "Trey..."

"I know, you have a man. I didn't forget."

"Yes, I do, and as a matter of fact, he's here tonight. I should go."

Trey pursed his lips, disappointment evident in his eyes. "Okay. Thanks for the invitation. My daughter and I had a great time."

"I'm glad you came. I'll see you around."

"You sure will."

Skye spent the next few minutes making her rounds to say

goodbye to staff and volunteers and some of the parents and actors and actresses from the play. Then she walked to where Ethan stood at the back, leaning against the wall, one hand in his pocket, legs crossed at the ankles. Despite the relaxed pose, she sensed tension in him, but he smiled as she approached and pushed away from the wall.

"Ready to go?" he asked.

"Yes."

He walked beside her, a hand at her lower back. On the way out they passed Janelle. The younger woman glanced sideways at Skye and smirked, silently reminding her Janelle had something she didn't.

The mixture of envy and anger was a volatile cocktail. Skye balled up her hands but quickly calmed her temper when the warning from Thresa popped into her head.

Calm down, she thought. Walking through the doors with Ethan, she relaxed her fingers and determined not to be bothered by Janelle's immature, petty behavior.

They climbed into the back of the limo and Halston took off.

"What did you think about the play?" Skye asked, tucking a strand of hair behind her ear and angling her body toward Ethan.

"The kids did a fantastic job. I never knew talking prehistoric animals could be so entertaining. You did a great job, sweetheart. You must be happy."

"Thank you, baby, I am," Skye said, smiling. "One of the volunteers suggested letting the rec area double as our theater, and it worked well, don't you think? We might do more plays." A light laugh skipped across her lips. "Emphasis on the word 'might.' The kids are excited about performing again, but who knows how they'll feel when the excitement wears off."

Ethan's eyes skimmed her outfit—figure-hugging jeans and a black T-shirt molded over her breasts.

"Who was the man talking to you back there, at the end?"

Skye blinked. The sudden change in topic took her by surprise. "Uh... a friend." Why did she feel guilty all of a sudden?

"Not one of the parents? A friend?" Ethan's eyes narrowed fractionally.

"More of an acquaintance, really. He owns the restaurant Thresa and I go to sometimes. Why?"

"He was standing rather close to you."

"Really? I don't think so." Skye brushed imaginary lint from her thigh.

Ethan caught her chin and forced her gaze to his. "I do."

She tugged her face from his grasp. "You're overreacting. He's an acquaintance, nothing more."

Ethan studied her in silence, a soft frown wrinkling his forehead. She maintained eye contact, well aware of his possessive streak and not wanting to create unnecessary problems.

Finally, his posture relaxed, and the moment passed. "I have bad news. I received a call today from my contact in China. She needs me to come over there and smooth out some issues."

Her heart sank. "What issues?"

"Nothing to concern yourself about."

Slighted by the abrupt way he closed off the conversation about business, Skye's lips tightened. She couldn't tell if he didn't think she could comprehend the intricacies of the problems he faced in real estate development, or if he simply wanted to keep her from worrying. She chose to believe the latter was the reason but deep down doubted that was the case.

She considered asking him point blank why he always shut her out of any substantive discussions about his business affairs, thus forcing a potentially tough conversation, but last time she asked a point blank question they ended up in a big fight—when she learned Ethan had no intention of marrying her.

"Unfortunately, I have to leave tonight," he added.

"*Tonight?*"

"It can't be helped. I wish I could cancel, but the deal is too important."

She hated he needed to leave so soon after they'd begun to mend their relationship. "How long will you be gone?"

"Seven days at the most."

She sighed, and the night's excitement tanked. She and Ethan had made headway in their relationship since the trip to Belize, but they still had a way to go.

"Well, if you have to go, you have to go."

"You're upset."

"Disappointed."

Ethan traveled all the time, but for some inexplicable reason, tonight's sudden departure stung like a death knell to their relationship. Skye folded her arms across her midsection and stared out the window. They cruised along at a moderate speed to their palatial home outside the city, whizzing by other cars and houses tucked behind trees that lined the highway.

She turned to look at him, but his attention was also focused outside the limousine.

"Are you happy, Ethan?"

"Of course, I'm happy."

"With me, I mean."

"Yes. What kind of question is that?"

Skye shrugged. "I don't know. Forget I asked," she said thickly.

A large hand covered her knee. "Sweetheart, I wish I didn't have to leave, but I do."

"I know."

"Do you? I'd much rather spend time with you than a bunch of suits on the other side of the world."

Ask me to come with you, she thought. But he wouldn't. He never did. One time she promised not to get in the way, and he still insisted on going alone.

"I'll make it up to you when I get back, okay?"

A faint smile. "How?"

"I..." His brow creased for a second. "I feel like I've missed the mark on the last few gifts, so you tell me. What do you want?"

Skye opened her mouth to answer and then stopped. In all honesty, what she really wanted he refused to give, so what was the point? Another pretty ring or necklace couldn't satisfy her desire to marry and start a family with him.

"I don't want anything," Skye said.

Then she stared out the window again.

Chapter Nineteen

Skye turned her face into the warm spray of the shower. The kids had done a great job, the parents in attendance were proud, and the advanced clips she viewed from the videographer captured the performance and the crowd's occasional laughter and applause at the end in vivid detail. Overall, the night had been a success.

She should be celebrating. Instead, she was an emotional wreck. She and Ethan needed to talk, but he was leaving for China tonight and could be gone for up to a week. She wanted to move past her feelings of hopelessness, but all she could think about was how her relationship lacked permanence.

Everything hit her at once. First Ignacio and Aunt Florence's comments, then Ethan's blunt rejection of marriage to her. Brunch and the disagreement in front of their friends, and finally the coup de grâce—Janelle's engagement news and mean-girl jab. She accomplished in six months what Skye couldn't in seven years. In a few years, Janelle and her new husband would be bragging about the latest antics of their kids, and all Skye would be able to brag about was another pair of diamond earrings.

Was she wrong for wanting it all—the lifestyle, the man, a family?

Suddenly, the tears started to fall. Placing her hands on the cold white marble of the shower stall, she let her head fall forward, shoulders shaking as she cried.

"Skye?"

To her horror, Ethan stood on the opposite side of the glass. She'd been so preoccupied with her own thoughts, she never heard him enter the bathroom.

He'd partially undressed, removing his jacket and vest, tie, and shoes.

Worry creased his brow as he opened the shower door. "Why are you crying?"

The anxiety in his voice called to something inside her. A need to be comforted and reassured. How could they not have been on the same page all along?

"I'm not. I'm..." She shook her head and swallowed hard, unable to finish the lie.

Ethan stepped into the shower.

"What are you doing? Your clothes are going to get soaked."

The lines of his chiseled face sharpened in concern. "Tell me what's wrong," he demanded.

"I wasn't crying," Skye insisted. Part of her wanted to hold on to some semblance of normalcy. Pretend her heart wasn't splitting in two and her world wasn't falling apart.

"Don't lie to me," Ethan said.

He cupped her face in both hands, holding her as if she were a delicate figurine he worried about breaking, gently forcing her to meet his gaze. There was no point in lying. He could read her like a book and always saw through her fibs.

"I need a moment." She grasped his wrists and lowered his hands from her face. "Could you give me a moment? Please."

Whenever she used that one little word, he always acquiesced. Perhaps she should try that with the marriage conversation. Marry me, please. Make me your wife, please. Let's start a family, *please*.

Ethan didn't move, and water pummeled the left side of his body, soaking his shirt, pants, and socks. "We talk when you get out," he said in a hard tone. Then he backed away and left her alone.

Tears sprang to Skye's eyes again as she finished her shower, washing her body with hands that twitched in an uncontrollable display of nerves.

Afterward, she knotted the belt of her fluffy pink robe around her waist and exited the bathroom. Ethan had changed into dark jeans and a polo shirt. At the moment, his attention was taken by the well-lit stone balcony outside the French doors.

Casually-dressed Ethan was as devastatingly handsome as business-dressed Ethan. The shirt's short sleeves showed off his muscular arms and the tattoo of a dollar sign on his right bicep. After he successfully rented out his first residential property—the gift from his stepfather—youthful excitement prompted him to get the ink.

He turned to her, frowning, as if he carried the world on his broad shoulders. After so much time together, she knew what he needed. A massage and his favorite drink—a glass of Cognac, neat. It was the drink in front of him when they met in the bar seven years ago. God, seven years ago. An eternity.

Normally, she brought the drink, massaged his shoulders, and encouraged him to relax. Only this time, *she* was the cause of his mental stress.

"I know you have to catch your flight," Skye said. Though he was taking his private jet, they had a flight plan to adhere to.

"I have a few minutes before I need to leave for the airport. Are you going to tell me why you were crying in the bathroom?"

Skye wrapped her arms around herself. "I have something to tell you, and I don't know how."

His body went rigid, as if bracing for impact. "Say what you have to say."

Skye swallowed. "It's time for us to take a break."

He looked at her in confusion. "What do you mean, take a break? A break from what?"

"A break from us. A break from our relationship."

Understanding dawned on his face, and his eyes took on a hard, flinty look. "That's ridiculous."

"I'm serious."

"Why?"

"I feel like I've been wasting my time all these years. I need time to process that, to think."

"You think our life together has been a waste? You're being emotional," he said dismissively.

"I am *not* being emotional."

"We returned from an amazing trip together just last week. What happened to prompt the tears and this conversation? Did you see someone with a baby? Did one of your friends back in California get married?"

He couldn't have been more casually cruel if he'd slapped her. "You can be such an asshole."

"You're calling *me* an asshole? You're the one talking about taking a break. I don't take breaks. If we're together, we're together, and if we're apart, then we're apart. There is no in-between." He glared at her.

"Fine, then we'll be apart." His flippant attitude turned her fear of talking to him into anger.

"Don't be a fool, Skye. Don't walk away from a perfectly good relationship because you're worried about what other people think."

"I thought we were moving toward something, and we're *not*. We've been together for *years*."

"Haven't they been good years?"

Skye's gaze dipped to the carpet beneath their feet. "Yes, they have," she admitted quietly.

She almost wished she hadn't gone to the graduation party because then she wouldn't have encountered Aunt Florence and her triggering words. But their conversation was the wakeup call she had needed, bringing to the forefront the topic she could hardly broach with herself. Her need for permanence. Her need for a family of her own. Her need to be more than Ethan's live-in girlfriend.

She would miss cuddling with him in the theater room and making love in the bed they shared. She would miss holidays with his family, nice dinners out, the lovely jewelry he gifted her from time to time, and the home they lived in. She'd be a fool to give all of that up. She knew that. Yet...

She lifted her gaze. The ache pulsing beneath her ribs wouldn't go away. Because it was *not* enough. None of it mattered because she loved Ethan and wanted to be his wife— and he made sure she understood that would never happen.

"If they've been good years, stop this foolishness about taking a break. What do you want? A piece of jewelry? Or would you rather a donation to your favorite charity?"

Gifts were his answer to every argument. She should have never allowed him to believe a pair of earrings fixed their problems.

Shoving her hands in the large pockets of the bathrobe, Skye said, "Don't. I don't want anything else from you."

"Why not?"

She paced away from him. "Because I'm tired of this. And yes, someone I know is not married, but she's engaged. After only *six* months."

"Their marriage probably won't last," he said.

"Or it will last forever."

"You are as close to me as any woman has ever been, and that should be enough."

"But it's not," Skye said, voice quivering.

Ethan walked over to her and grasped her shoulders. "What you and I have is good. It's strong. It's special. You have access to almost every aspect of my life."

"I know, I'm lucky, and asking for more sounds greedy."

"Not greedy, misguided. That piece of paper means nothing. Look at us. Look at everything we have. Remember what Amy said about Erica and Tom? They're getting a divorce. After fifteen years. My mother and Benicio are divorced, and they were married for more than twenty years."

"I want a family."

"You're part of my family."

"I want my own family. I want children. Do you want children?" For the second time that night, she thought how Ethan would be an amazing father, and she wanted to be the mother of his children.

"Eventually. I..." He rubbed the back of his neck. "If I had them, I'd want them with you, but marriage is out of the question."

Her heart cracked in two. "Then we're at an impasse."

"No, we're not. There is always a way to negotiate past any problem," Ethan said.

Of course he would see the conversation as a negotiation,

akin to a business deal hitting a snag. All he needed to do was smooth out the wrinkles and everything would be fine. She'd shut up, and they'd go back to the status quo.

"You need to leave for China," Skye reminded him.

He grasped her upper arms again. "We'll talk when I get back."

"Okay. Go."

He kissed her forehead, and she held back the urge to cling to him, to beg him for what she needed. But she had her pride.

"We'll figure this out. We have to find a way to compromise. I do that all the time in business." He sounded so reasonable.

Skye nodded but refused to look at him. She kept her eyes focused on the neckline of his shirt.

Ethan tilted up her chin and searched her face.

"I love you. We belong together. We are not taking a break. Leaving me is not an option on the table."

More business language.

Skye didn't flinch. "I hear you, loud and clear."

He kissed her, and the warmth of his lips dragged her closer. The taste of him was exquisite and sent a quiver of longing through her belly. She accepted the three torturous licks of his tongue and the tugging pull of his teeth on her lower lip. Smoothing her hand up the inside of his shirt, she traced the ridges of abs of steel covered in silken mahogany flesh.

"I need you." His voice shook a little as he whispered the words against her neck. "You've told me hundreds of times that you're mine."

Knowing what she had to do, Skye closed her eyes. She'd never hear his warm voice in her ear again, demanding she say that she belonged to him. She'd never again breathlessly pant, "I'm yours. Oh god, Ethan, yes, yes, I'm yours!"

"Did you lie to me when you said those words?" he asked.

Skye shook her head. "No."

"Good." He sounded relieved. "I'll call you when I land in Beijing." He kissed her cheek.

Skye didn't reply.

He searched her eyes, and she looked back at him unflinchingly. Whatever he was looking for, he didn't find. He kissed her one last time and left.

Skye removed her robe and climbed onto his side of the bed, falling asleep to the scent of him filling her nostrils.

The next morning, she packed up her personal effects, leaving behind all of the designer items. She liked dressing up and looking good for him but no longer needed them because she and Ethan would no longer be attending events together, and she would certainly not be attending events that required such elegant attire by herself. Lower-priced clothing sufficed for a life without Ethan.

A member of the household staff helped take her boxes and bags downstairs and place them in a rented trailer hitched to the back of her Lexus.

In the driveway, she swiped away tears with trembling fingers and climbed into her vehicle. The servants wouldn't tell Ethan she'd left. They were known for their discretion and didn't interfere in his personal life. Nonetheless, she hoped none of them suffered any adverse consequences for not alerting him about her departure.

Skye drove away from seven and a half years with a heavy heart. Leaving was the right decision. No point in delaying the inevitable. She refused to waste another day in this dead end relationship and would not give Ethan any more years.

Chapter Twenty

E than stalked into the master bedroom and planted his feet in the middle of the carpet. The stillness in the room set off alarm bells in his head.

He rushed over to Skye's dressing room and flicked on the light. Right away he knew some of her belongings were gone. While in Beijing he'd suspected she might leave. They didn't speak once during his trip and only exchanged a few texts. His suspicions were confirmed the minute he walked into the house by the way Mona's gaze didn't quite meet his eyes.

Ethan strolled to the island in the middle of the closet and yanked open several of the drawers. She took the less expensive clothing items and accessories—hair clips, belts, scarves, but not the five-thousand-dollar dresses or two-thousand-dollar four-inch heels.

He shoved aside her slacks and tapped the wall behind them on the right side. It popped open to expose a safe built into the wall. He pressed his thumb to the pad and after a few seconds the latch opened. Jewelry adorned with diamonds and other precious gemstones glimmered in their glass cases. She

125

didn't take any of the jewelry he gave her, though she swore she loved the pieces. Then he saw the stack of credit cards. She had left those too.

Ethan slammed the safe shut as cold anger coursed through his veins and marched out of the bedroom door.

"Mona!" he bellowed. His voice echoed in the hallway as if he were in the belly of a cave.

His housekeeper came scurrying toward him. "Yes, Mr. Connor."

She folded her hands in front of her. Mona was not usually so docile, so she must be aware of what he was about to ask.

"When did she leave?" he asked.

"Friday afternoon."

Skye exchanged texts with him as if nothing had changed the entire time he was gone. Lying to him. Deceiving him.

"That was the last time you saw her?"

"Yes. She never came back."

She must have been planning to leave him all along, to move out so quickly, as soon as his back was turned.

"Thank you," Ethan said, retreating into the bedroom.

He thought he heard her softly say, "I'm sorry."

His heart seized. That sounded like pity.

He swung to speak harsh words to deflect the sympathy in her voice, but she was already gone. With clenched fists, he crossed the floor toward the French doors. He needed air.

When he saw an envelope on the table beside the bed, he pulled up short. He snatched it up and removed the small card. Skye's feminine, loopy handwriting was inside. The note was short and simple.

I'm sorry, Ethan. I love you, but I can't do this anymore.
Skye

He crushed the card in his fist and stared at the empty bed —the bed he and she shared. He'd rushed back from overseas, making concessions he normally didn't make, to cut the trip short so he could get back to her—like some kind of love sick pup.

Yet she wasn't here. She had left him. For her, he had opened his home, his heart, and his wallet, and this is how she repaid him.

Taking long strides out the door, he dialed her number. After three rings, she picked up.

"Hello?" she answered cautiously.

"Where are you?"

"Ethan—"

"We are not done. Where are you, Skye?" He made haste down the staircase and crossed the foyer to the front door.

She didn't answer.

"Do you think I can't find you in five minutes? Tell me where you are. *Now.*"

He hauled open the front door with unnecessary force and walked outside. Halston was in the driveway vacuuming the interior of the limo and looked up when Ethan exited.

"You tried your best, but our relationship can't be repaired. We want different things."

Ethan gazed out across his multi-acre property, his grip on the phone so tight he was close to crushing it. "Where. Are. You."

Seconds ticked by, and he waited.

Finally, Skye made a sound of resignation. "I'm at a hotel."

"Which hotel?"

"The Winthrop, downtown."

"Don't move. I'm on my way."

Ethan shoved the phone in his pocket. "Take me to The Winthrop Hotel downtown," he said to Halston. He opened his own door and climbed into the back.

Skye might think walking out meant they were done, but he would make sure she understood that was not the case.

* * *

"You lied to me." Ethan stood in the hallway outside Skye's room, face tight, jaw rigid.

She had dreaded his visit ever since he called and said he was on his way over.

"I didn't lie."

"You led me to believe you'd be at the house when I came back from overseas."

"You said we could talk when you came back, and I agreed. I never said I would stay."

Ethan pushed his way into the room, and she closed the door, taking a fortifying breath to deal with the difficult conversation ahead. She did not regret leaving, but she wished he didn't look so good. She couldn't help but appreciate his casually elegant appearance in a white shirt and black slacks. No wonder she'd fallen into bed with him so easily the night they met.

She'd had plenty of time to think over the past few days and analyzed their relationship through a new lens. She had slept with Ethan the first night they met. Maybe she'd been too easy. She moved in with him eighteen months into the relationship. Maybe that made him become comfortable with her and think she was willing to settle.

"You never said you would leave either, but you did, sneaking out of my house as soon as my back was turned."

"*Your* house?" The muscles around her heart contracted with pain.

"You know what I mean. It's your house too."

"Sure it is. I told you we were at an impasse, you insisted

we weren't, but I know the truth. You won't give me what I want, and I won't accept anything less."

"I never lied to you. I never pretended I was going to marry you."

"You're right, you didn't."

"So why move out, and what was the point of leaving behind everything I gave you?"

She knew Ethan. Her rejection of his gifts cut to the core of his role as a man and her provider. "There was no point. I don't need those things anymore."

"Do you think you can force me into marriage?"

She laughed, but there was no humor to the sound. "I'm not so foolish to believe I can force the great Ethan Connor to do anything he doesn't want to do. I know you're not going to change your mind, but neither am I."

"How will you survive? I've provided for you all these years."

"For your information, I'm not a charity case. Consider yourself relieved of the burden of taking care of me."

Ethan always put the women in his life on a pedestal and treated them like queens, including his female employees. He offered generous bonuses and compensation packages to all his employees but was particularly considerate to his female staff. As long as his generosity wasn't abused, there was no end to the lavish gifts.

Some people might see his behavior as paternalistic or sexist, but his decisions were steeped in the struggles he saw his mother experience when he was a child. He never forgot those lean years.

For that reason, he protected the women in his life and found ways to honor them and show his appreciation. He named a hotel after his mother; his personal assistant, Layla, lived rent-free in a building of lofts he owned; his executive assistant, Daria, was a single mother and didn't have to pay for her son's college education and pretty much possessed a bottomless petty cash fund to treat herself to the occasional lunch and send herself flowers at his expense.

He treated Skye no differently. In fact, she was perhaps the greatest recipient of his generosity. But their relationship had run its course. Keeping the credit cards would have been in bad taste, but leaving behind the clothes was a way for her to leave her life with him behind.

"You're letting outside forces affect *our* relationship. Married doesn't mean happy," Ethan said. "I am as devoted to you as any couple with a piece of paper between them."

"The piece of paper is binding."

His eyebrows came together in a flare of anger. "What difference does it make?"

"It makes a difference to me!" she screamed. "It's a promise, and you of all people should understand the importance of having something in writing. 'If it's not in writing, it's not binding.' Those are *your* words. Look, I know your marriage was a mess—"

"You don't know anything about my marriage." He interrupted in a clipped, wooden tone.

A pulse of frustration tightened her lips. Except during their trip to Belize, every time they talked about his marriage, he lost his temper. Their conversations about Joanne had been thankfully rare, but each time the topic arose, he expressed extremely negative emotions. He so obviously despised her. She had never met his ex but had seen pictures of her and knew a little based on conversations with Monica and the bits of information Ethan shared.

"You're right, I don't. Because except for what you told me in Belize, you always shut me out. Just like you shut me out when it comes to business. I host your parties, but anything concerning business, you go alone or take Layla." At one time she'd thought he was having an affair with his pretty PA. "Why? Because you think I'm too dumb to understand what's going on?"

"Of course not," he said irritably.

"Then why?"

"Because my business doesn't concern you." He spoke slowly, eye contact steady.

A sharp pain lanced her heart. Another wall.

"This game you're playing doesn't make sense, Skye."

"It's not a game. I'm not coming back to you."

"Listen to me—"

"No, *you* listen. We're not negotiating. I'm not coming back to you."

"Because I won't marry you."

"Yes. I think it's best we both find people who can give us what we want."

Fury flashed in his eyes. "You will never find another man who can give you what I can."

"I doubt that, but if it's true, then it's also true you will never find another woman who can give you what I can."

An indefinable emotion crossed his stony features before his face fell back into disinterested lines. "Last chance, Skye."

She marched over to the door and pulled it open. "I've been on my own since I was seventeen. I don't need anything from you."

The left corner of his mouth twitched with humor, which infuriated her. She narrowed her eyes and glowered at him.

"Don't pretend you don't need me. We've meant too much to each other to throw away our relationship on a whim—like it means nothing at all. Clearly I shouldn't have been so dismissive of your need for a break. How much time do you need?"

"What part of 'I'm not coming back to you' do you not understand? The break is no longer on the table."

"Thirty days should be enough time for you to sort through your feelings and come to the right decision," Ethan said, as if she hadn't spoken. He walked slowly toward her.

Instead of going through the door, he stopped directly in front of her, forcing her to tilt her head back to glare at him. A tremor of longing rattled in her chest when she gazed up into his dark eyes. She missed him already and hoped and prayed the wrenching pain ceased soon enough.

He moved so swiftly, she didn't have time to dodge his mouth. Long fingers wrapped around her upper arms and dragged her to him. She expected a brutal kiss but received a tender caress, causing her fingers to curl into his soft shirt.

Need flooded her core as Ethan took his time kissing her, his mouth slanting over hers as his tongue slid through her mouth in a decadent, snakelike dance. When he finally pulled back, his teeth plucked at her lower lip, and to her dismay she let out a shaky breath of discontent at his withdrawal. Why couldn't her wayward body behave? Her need for him was terribly inconvenient.

The heat of embarrassment stained her cheeks, and she put as much distance between them as she could in the small entryway.

"No need to be ashamed. You know that's the way it is between us. I can't resist touching you, and you can't resist my touch."

He dropped another kiss to her mouth, a quick peck this time—but she managed to keep her lips stiff.

Ethan looked down at her from his superior height, unperturbed by her rejection. "You want to think, I'll give you space to think. You can have your break. Thirty days." He forced her chin higher with one long finger. "Then I'm coming to get you." He delivered the words calmly and without a hint of emotion.

Skye didn't move, remaining very still until he walked out. After he left, she slumped against the door and closed her eyes.

Typical. He didn't believe she was serious about leaving him for good and thought he could overrun her decision with talk of a break.

Well, she would show him. The real estate shark who won at any costs was about to meet his match.

Chapter Twenty-One

Ethan couldn't remember the last time he came to his mother's house for Sunday dinner. By the number of cars in the driveway, she had a full house.

He let himself into the home in time to see Audra's kids—Tracy and Damon Junior—racing down opposite staircases in the foyer.

His eight-year-old nephew reached the bottom first. "I win!" he crowed.

"I was close," seven-year-old Tracy said.

Ignoring his sister, Damon ran over to Ethan. "Hi, Uncle Ethan!"

Ethan gave them both a hug.

"Where's Skye?" Tracy asked.

He fully expected to hear the same question asked several times and intended to keep the answers short.

"She's not coming today," he replied.

"Aww. I wanted to show her my poem." Tracy stuck out her lower lip.

"Don't be a baby. She'll look at your poem next time," Damon said.

"Don't call her a baby," Ethan said.

"Sorry," Damon muttered, not looking sorry at all. Tracy smirked at him.

Damon's eyes lit up. "Uncle Ethan, guess what? I got an A on my math test."

"You did? So if I tell you to count in multiples of five up to thirty, what's your answer?"

Standing ramrod straight, as if saluting a sergeant, the little boy recited the numbers. "Five, ten, fifteen, twenty, twenty-five, thirty."

"And what's five times two?" Ethan asked.

"Ten!"

"All right. Good job. How much do I owe you for your A?"

"Five dollars," the boy answered excitedly, bouncing on his feet.

Audra started down the long staircase, and Ethan acknowledged her with a nod.

"Five dollars?" He removed his wallet from his pocket and held up a twenty. "This is all I have."

Damon snatched the bill. "I'll take it! Thanks, Uncle Ethan. Look, Mommy, I have twenty dollars!" He raced off with his sister running behind him.

Audra took the last few steps to the bottom. She wore a white dress with flowers all over it and her hair flipped up at the ends. She looked every bit the homemaker she touted herself to be on her lifestyle website.

"You're going to go broke paying him for good grades," she said.

"I'll survive. Where is everybody?"

"Mom wanted to take advantage of the nice weather, so everyone is outside on the terrace. Skye's not with you?"

"No. Is Damon here?"

Audra shook her head. "He's out of town."

They made their way outside. Two tables covered with white tablecloths contained the food and drinks. Next to them a long table surrounded by plenty of chairs was set up for the family to eat.

"There he is!" Ignacio said, placing roasted chicken on his plate with tongs.

"Smells good." Ethan surveyed the choices.

The spread included mashed potatoes, roasted chicken, his mother's famous macaroni and cheese required at almost every Sunday meal, and different vegetables. In addition, the chef on hand prepared made-to-order birria tacos, and at the end of one of the tables, carrot cake, pumpkin pie, and mini cheesecakes beckoned anyone with a sweet tooth. If Skye were here, she'd be all over the cheesecakes.

Pain cut into his chest, and he gritted his teeth to curtail the agony of missing her.

Rose approached Ethan and squeezed his arm. "Hi, honey. Where's Skye?" She looked behind them as if expecting Skye to suddenly appear.

"She's not coming."

Her brow furrowed with concern. "Is she sick?"

"No." Ethan picked up a plate and added a piece of chicken.

An unnatural silence forced him to turn around. All adult eyes were on him. The kids chattered in a corner, and his sixteen-year-old niece, Kerilyn, sat at the table with a phone and ear buds, bobbing her head to music no one else could hear.

Monica placed her hands on her hips. "What did you do?"

"What makes you think I did something?" Ethan asked.

"Because you did!"

He glared at her. "I didn't come here to be attacked. I came to enjoy a meal with my family."

Benicio approached, arms raised to calm the tempers before they flared out of control. "Everyone, let's get our plates and eat this delicious meal like a family. Rosa and the staff prepared all this food for us, including birria tacos because I requested them." He squeezed his ex-wife's shoulders from behind.

"We used Bruno's recipe," Ethan's mother said.

"Then they will be delicious. Come on, *pequeños*, get your food so we can say grace and eat. *Tengo hambre.*"

"I'm hungry too, *abuelo.*" Tracy squeezed between Ethan and Benicio in the line and held out her plate.

"Here, let me give you some chicken. What else would you like?" Benicio asked.

Ethan continued piling food on his plate and then sat at the table with his family. Ignacio and Maxwell beside him, Benicio and Rose at opposite ends, Audra between her two youngest, and Monica sitting closest to Benicio.

They all held hands, Benicio said grace, and they dived into the food. Conversation flowed as they caught up on each other's lives.

Ethan skirted the topic of his relationship with Skye, sticking to the positive results of his trip to China and the progress on the Horizon development.

"This is delicious." Benicio held up a half-eaten taco stuffed full of tender, juicy meat.

Rose smiled, shaking her head. "You're so easy to please."

He chuckled, eyes twinkling as he gazed across the table at her. "Don't I always say the simple pleasures are the most enjoyable in life?"

Heads nodded around the table.

"Anybody home?" a male voice called.

Suddenly, Thiago appeared in the doorway and stepped

onto the terrace. He grinned as surprised cries went up from the group. Tracy and Damon jumped up, screaming, "Uncle Thiago!"

Rose's mouth fell open, and she shot a glance at Benicio. "Did you know he was coming?"

A smug expression on his face, Benicio responded, "I did. It was a surprise."

Rose stood up and squeezed Thiago in a warm embrace, and he hugged her back with the same energy. "Oh, it's so good to see you." They rocked from side to side.

"So you skipped my graduation party but you can make time for Mom's Sunday dinner?" Maxwell teased, pulling his brother into a hug.

"If anything can get me to come home, it's Mama Rosa's cooking," Thiago said.

"Stop it," Rose said, blushing. "Let me fix you a plate. Sit next to me." She patted the empty chair where Damon would have been sitting next to his daughter, if he were present.

"How was your flight?" Benicio asked.

"Long, and I'm glad to be home." Thiago ran his fingers through his short, dark hair.

"How long will you be here?" Monica asked.

"A few weeks at least. I'm doing preliminary work for one of our clients."

When Benicio expanded his business empire beyond the entertainment industry, his pursuits included real estate, retail stores, a consulting business, and ownership in a high-priced tequila brand. Thiago ran the consulting arm of his father's business.

Audra set a glass of iced tea in front of him.

"I never get this kind of treatment when I come back," Ignacio said in a wounded voice.

"I'm special," Thiago returned.

"I'm just happy we're all here together. This was a lovely surprise." Rose looked across the table at Benicio, who smiled at her. "Eat, eat. There's plenty of food."

Two hours passed with much laughter, teasing, and minor arguments. As Ethan sipped his iced tea, he felt empty despite enjoying himself. Skye should be here. She looked forward to these get-togethers and liked learning new recipes from Rose. On more than one occasion she expressed regret at not spending more time in the kitchen with her mother before she passed.

Night fell and everyone migrated inside. Thiago went to bed early, tired from the long flight. Benicio, Maxwell, and Kerilyn watched a movie in the basement theater room.

Ethan didn't know where Monica disappeared to, but he helped Audra take the kids up to the guest room after they had fallen asleep on chairs in the great room. She carried Tracy, and he carried Damon up the stairs and placed them in bed in the room that used to be Monica and Audra's. Boy band posters no longer decorated the walls. Instead, tasteful art and neutral décor turned the bedroom into a haven for guests.

Ethan tucked in his nephew, gazing down at the little boy as he slept fitfully. He looked content, the way a child should. No worries in the world. If he ever became a father, he wanted the same for his own children.

He hadn't thought about having children much, but the idea did cross his mind on occasion. The possibility seemed further away now because of the rift between him and Skye, but he was determined not to let her get away. Just like he told her, their separation was temporary. Maybe when they came back together, they could discuss the possibility of having children.

He and his sister quietly exited the room and stood in the hallway.

"Every time I go in that room, I remember how Monica and I used to have to share it and how she was always in my business. I used to be so jealous of you and Bruno because you were the oldest and had your own rooms."

"That's the privilege of being born first. If you had wanted your own room, you should have been born first."

Audra folded her arms across her chest and pursed her lips. "Ha. You're funny. Are you going to the Johnson Foundation fundraiser next week? I'm going to pass this year."

"You missed last year."

"I know, but I have a million things to do. I'll send a donation later."

"I'll be there," Ethan said.

"You and Skye?" Audra asked, trying not to sound nosy while obviously fishing for information.

"I'm going alone." The last five years in a row, he and Skye attended the annual fundraiser together. He hated the thought of sitting at the table without her, but this was one of the few events he liked attending because the Johnsons did good work.

"Oh." Audra tilted her head to the side, studying him with concern in her eyes. "Are you and Skye okay?"

"We hit a rough patch," he admitted. "It's temporary. What about you and Damon? He missed the graduation party and now today..."

Audra broke eye contact. "We're fine. He's just busy. You know how that is."

"Yes, I do," Ethan replied. She was obviously lying, but he didn't push.

"I'll see you later."

They hugged.

"Get some rest. You look tired."

"I will, and I am," Audra said with a little laugh.

They parted ways, and Ethan went down the long hallway

to the top of the stairs. His mother was coming up, stifling a yawn with her hand. "You're leaving?"

"No, I'm going to stay and leave after breakfast tomorrow. I'm going to get some water."

"Good. I had a full house tonight. If Bruno and Skye and Damon were here, it would've been better, but it's hard to get everyone together at one time with so many different schedules."

"Yes."

Rose touched his face. "I hope whatever you and Skye are going through, you work it out."

His mother possessed an uncanny ability to read people.

"We will. We had an argument, that's all. I won't let her slip through my fingers."

"That's what I wanted to hear. Have a good night, honey."

She disappeared down the hall, and Ethan stuffed his hands in his pockets as he slowly descended the stairs.

He and Skye had been separated for thirteen days already.

He was miserable but resolved to keep his word and give her space.

Seventeen more days to go.

Chapter Twenty-Two

"I don't understand, I have good credit."

Skye paced the courtyard of the learning center with the phone attached to her ear. Another property manager was turning her down for an apartment. Last week she was certain she'd be moving into her first choice, Midtown Towers. The luxury apartments offered a wide range of amenities, including a concierge service and a state-of-the-art gym. Then they called to say they no longer had any vacancies, and she'd have to be put on a waiting list.

The woman on this call told her only seconds before that she did not qualify for their apartment due to lack of credit history. Granted, Skye hadn't needed new credit in quite some time. She had lived with Ethan for over five years and almost exclusively used his credit cards, but she did have *some* credit from when she used to live on her own.

"I'm sorry ma'am, but you'll have to look elsewhere," the woman said in her nasal twang.

"I can pay a larger deposit if you think—"

"I'm sorry, Miss Thorpe. I wish we could help, but we can't.

I suggest you try another property. Perhaps you'll have better luck there. Another potential renter has entered the office. I have to go. Bye-bye!"

"Wait—" Skye heard nothing but a dial tone.

Another dead end. She stared at the phone and released a low cry of frustration. None of this made sense. Before she and Ethan had become involved, she had rented her own apartment and... *Ethan.*

He wouldn't.

"He would," Skye said to herself.

She marched into the building and stopped at the front. Thresa was on the phone.

"I'm taking an early lunch. I'll be back in an hour or so," she told her.

Skye didn't wait for a reply and stormed out of the building. A short while later, she was hustling down the sidewalk toward Ethan's building. She paused at the entrance, slightly winded from her brisk walk, and gazed up at the forty-story monstrosity planted in the middle of the block, a glaring testament to the ego of the man sitting at the very top. It wasn't enough for Ethan to have the tallest building for miles around. He'd also added his name in giant silver letters on the outside.

Connor International Industries.

She sighed. His ego was the least of her problems.

Squaring her shoulders, Skye passed through the rotating door. The atrium-style interior allowed a vast amount of sunlight to enter, and the sun's rays fed the growth of strategically placed trees and shrubs, giving the impression of being outside even though inside a building. In front of her, escalators to the left and right led up to glass-walled offices on the first six floors.

People milled around, most dressed in business attire and only sparing her a brief glance before hurrying to the bank of elevators or exiting through the doors she'd come through. A security guard and a woman dressed in a sharp blue suit answered questions at the Information Desk.

Taking a deep breath, she went toward the elevator and smiled at the five people inside before hitting the button for the top floor.

She whispered a quick prayer that she could reason with Ethan and say all the right words to convince him to rescind his actions and leave her the hell alone.

On floor forty, a receptionist greeted Skye and called back to Ethan's office.

She glanced around, noting the sleek interior. Despite the length of their relationship, she had only been to his office a handful of times because there hadn't been any reason for her to come by. Whenever they went out, he usually sent Halston to pick her up at the mansion or the suite at The Rose Hotel.

"Miss Thorpe, you can go back. Do you need me to escort you?" the receptionist asked.

"I know the way. Thank you."

Ethan's executive assistant met her with a guarded smile. They'd been friendly over the years, chatting now and again when she called for Ethan, but she understood Daria's loyalty was to her boss.

She escorted Skye immediately into his office, and the door closed quietly behind her. Ethan sat behind his huge black desk, window at his back, looking like an overlord receiving a subject.

"I'm sure you know why I'm here," she said, walking forward.

His eyes followed her movements, and heat cruised across her skin. She hadn't seen him in two weeks, and her jumpy nerves made her uneasy in his presence.

"I've tried to move into three luxury apartments, and none of them will have me. I find that very odd."

"Are you accusing me of something?"

Spreading her fingers on the black desk, Skye locked eyes with Ethan. "Why are you sabotaging my chances of getting an apartment? Don't pretend you don't know what I'm talking about."

He slowly tapped a pen on the desk. "I admit that I made a few phone calls and had my management company send some emails regarding your living options."

"You're not even denying it." She straightened.

"I would never lie to you. You know that."

"What's the endgame?"

"I gave you thirty days."

"And I told you I wasn't coming back."

"You said you needed time to think, and I'm giving you time to think." He was as cool as a popsicle. "If you rent an apartment and lock yourself into a lease, that could unduly influence your decision making. I want you to be able to think clearly and rationally."

"Well thank you so very much, but you can't influence everyone in the city. I *will* find a place, even if it means I have to drive farther out."

"I would hate for you to inconvenience yourself like that. As you well know, the real estate rental community is surprisingly small. There are a few major players who own multiple properties. Many of us, if not friends, are at least colleagues. We help each other when we can."

"I never thought you would be the kind of man to do something like this."

"You know exactly what kind of man I am."

Sad but true. His actions shouldn't come as a surprise. Ethan could be tender and definitely generous, but he also had a ruthless side. She'd once heard him threaten to ruin someone he thought had double-crossed him.

"You're right. I guess I never thought you would do something like this to me."

"Men do terrible things when they're desperate," he said quietly.

He rose from the chair, and tension worked its way through her muscles. She eyed him as he approached her on the other side of the desk. Inserting his hands in his pockets, he gazed down at her from over six feet.

Skye stood within touching distance, way too close. Tension danced in her stomach.

His eyes took a leisurely stroll from head to toe, causing her breasts to tingle and between her thighs to pulse with want.

"Let's talk about your living situation over dinner."

Skye let out a rude, loud laugh. "You must be out of your mind. The only way I'll have dinner with you is if you force me."

"We both know I've never had to force you to do anything." His voice dropped an octave. "You were always a ready and willing participant."

Twin flames of heat burned her cheeks.

True enough, she had found him intriguing from the very first night. An enigma. A polished professional who, it turned out, had a hidden talent for playing the piano because his mother had insisted her children learn some "culture." She'd come to know him so well that night, climbing into bed with him seemed the logical next step after spending hours together eating, talking, and laughing with comfortable ease. That man was nowhere to be found at the moment.

"I won't waste my breath talking to you anymore because it's obvious you won't listen. You insist that I'm coming back, even though I've told you more than once that I'm not."

"You don't just throw away seven years together like it's nothing."

"I'm not the one throwing away our time together. You are."

A muscle in his jaw twitched as he fought for control. "You were the one who left, Skye. *Not* me. All I'm asking you to do is stop and consider what you're giving up, and you'll agree your behavior is ridiculous."

"Ridiculous? That's the problem. You don't respect me or my feelings. I told you what I wanted, and you refuse to give it to me. What I did was sensible, or I'd be stuck in a dead-end relationship for another seven years. I will find a place to live— even if I have to drive all the way out to Conyers. I'll approach individual landlords. I'll do whatever it takes because I am not coming back to live in your house."

"Our house," he corrected.

She laughed bitterly. "No, you said it the right way the first time. *Your* house. Good. Bye." She took angry strides across the floor.

"You're wasting your time. You'll have to break the lease when you return home."

"Fuck you, Ethan," she said without turning around.

"I wish."

He spoke softly, but Skye heard him. Her breath caught, and she swung around near the door, a soft throb of heat beating at the apex of her thighs.

Tight-lipped, she exited the office and slammed the door on her way out.

Ethan stared at the closed door for a long time and then stalked over to the window. He dragged a hand down his face as he gazed unseeing at the landscape of buildings.

Despite their angry words, he had been happy to see her. He spent less time at home now because without Skye, the house seemed more like an empty shell than the peaceful retreat it transformed into because of her.

She looked like she'd lost a little weight, but overall she was the same Skye, and being so close to her turned him on. His balls ached. He'd had to stuff his hands in his pockets to keep from reaching for her.

This might very well be the longest thirty days of his life.

Chapter Twenty-Three

On her lunch break, Skye went to see a single-family home near the learning center but waffled on whether or not it was a viable option. The two-bedroom bungalow needed repairs, which the homeowner said would be completed before she moved in. She thanked him for taking the time to show her the property but left without filling out an application.

As she pulled her car into the parking lot outside the learning center, her phone rang. She smiled when she saw the name on the screen and answered. "Hi, Amy. This is a nice surprise." Amy didn't usually call in the middle of the day.

Tucking the phone between her shoulder and ear, Skye maneuvered out of the car and braced for a long afternoon. The learning center was very busy. Janelle quit a few days ago, stating she needed time to plan her wedding. Skye wished she could say good riddance, but her absence meant more work for her and Thresa until a new person could be hired.

"I know, but Brian and I are planning a party on very short

notice—a week from Friday, to be exact, and I'm calling because I want to make sure you and Ethan can come."

Just hearing his name made her stomach clench.

Skye punched in her code at the door. "Amy, Ethan and I are no longer together."

Amy gasped. "You and Ethan split?"

Skye was surprised Amy didn't know since she knew all the gossip. "Yes. Several weeks ago."

"I had no idea. You two were one of those couples I assumed would eventually..."

Skye winced, finishing the sentence in her head. *Get married.*

"I mean, I—"

"It's okay, Amy. Ethan and I were together for a long time, and I was very happy, but he and I want different things. We grew apart."

"I'm so sorry to hear that. All the more reason why you need to come to this party. I'm handling the guest list, so there's nothing to worry about. Anyone not on my list is not invited and therefore not attending. Please come."

"Who's going to be there and what's the occasion?" She waved hello at Thresa as she sat down at her desk.

"Mostly familiar faces, and no special occasion. We need some grown-up entertainment because we haven't thrown a party in so long. The grandparents are on babysitting duty again, which means drinking and staying up as late as we want instead of staying up late because we can't get a constantly crying baby to go to sleep."

"Thanks for the invitation, and I wish I could say yes, but..."

"Please come. I'd love to see you, and you can bring a date if you want—I mean, if you're seeing someone already."

"I'm not... well, I could bring a friend, I guess." Trey's smiling face came to mind.

"Bring him!"

"He's more like an acquaintance."

"Bring. Him."

"I'll think about it. But if I did bring someone, wouldn't that be awkward for Brian? He and Ethan aren't just business colleagues, they're friends."

"I promise you have nothing to worry about. Let me handle Brian."

Skye hesitated, still unsure, but she needed to start living again. "In that case... yes, I'll be there. Probably by myself, though."

"Yay! I'll text you the details. Can't wait to see you."

After she hung up, Skye experienced a small sense of satisfaction. She hadn't done much except stay in the hotel room since she moved out of Ethan's house. She'd done a remarkable job so far holding her tattered life together in the face of their breakup, but what she saw on television last night broke her. She couldn't believe Ethan would do something so callous.

She realized with a start that Thresa was talking.

"What did you say?" she asked.

Thresa cast a sympathetic look across her desk. "Did you hear anything I said?"

Skye sighed. "I'm so sorry, no, I didn't."

"Are you thinking about Ethan?"

Skye dropped her gaze. "As always." She swallowed past the lump in her throat.

"You miss him," Thresa said.

"Ironic, since I'm the one who wanted to split up. The way he talks makes me sound unreasonable. We have a great life, so why leave?"

"Only you can answer that question, but in my experience,

anything that bothers you only becomes worse with time. It's not going to get any easier."

"I know you're right." Being without him was so hard, made harder by what she saw the other night. "I saw him on the news the other night," she said in a low voice.

"Doing what?" Thresa asked.

"He was at a fundraiser with some... woman." She bit back the urge to call the other woman out of her name. "Could you toss me a candy bar?"

"Sure." Thresa rummaged in her basket and tossed a candy bar across the room to Skye.

She bit into the chocolate and enjoyed the sweet taste mixed with nuts, a mild comfort to her bruised heart.

She didn't tell Thresa about the storm of jealousy that erupted inside her at seeing Ethan with another woman on his arm. He looked irritated when the reporter placed a mic in his face right before he went into the ballroom where the event was taking place. She'd been to the Johnson Foundation fundraisers with him for the past five years in a row. He hated the media attention and usually slipped in unnoticed and let attendees who liked the limelight talk to the reporters.

This time he hadn't been so lucky, and when Skye saw him with that woman, fears she didn't know existed bubbled to the surface. In such a short time he had already replaced her. Knowing that woman might join him at home in the bed they used to share made her ill.

"What are you going to do?" Thresa asked.

"There's nothing I can do. He's moved on." She bit off another piece of chocolate.

It was hard to explain how she knew that so definitively, but there was another reason seeing Ethan hit so hard.

Early in their relationship, she gave him a gold watch with a brown leather band and diamonds studding the face. She'd wanted to give him something nice, and the timepiece cost a small fortune. Not as much as one from Patek Philippe, his preferred brand, but enough to make her feel she were buying him something of value. Except she learned a flashy diamond-studded watch wasn't his style and had been embarrassed by her gaffe.

She offered to return the watch and buy a different one, but Ethan insisted on keeping it. Then, a few weeks later, he wore a tan suit to an event, and the watch was on his wrist. All of his suits up to that point had been navy, charcoal, or black. Light-colored suits were not part of his style. She later learned he instructed his stylist to incorporate lighter colors into his wardrobe so he'd have occasion to wear the watch.

She had probably fallen deeper in love with him the day he wore that suit with the watch she gave him, because his actions demonstrated that, despite his hard exterior, Ethan had a soft spot for her.

He wore a tan suit to the Johnson Foundation event, but the watch wasn't on his wrist. Something so small gutted her as she listened to him answer the reporter's questions in a short clip at the hotel.

The omission could have been an oversight, but she doubted it. She knew. He hadn't worn the timepiece because it reminded him of her. *I'm coming to get you.* His words didn't mean anything. He'd already cut her out of his life.

"Is there anything I can do?" Thresa asked.

"No. I have to sort this out. Let's talk about something else."

Skye insisted on talking about other topics, like the kids and the positive feedback they continued to receive about the play. The write up in the county paper had praised the center and included a photo. The kids squealed when they saw their faces in the paper.

Their newfound popularity prompted an acting club to

offer to send volunteers to help with the next production, and an African dance troupe said they'd teach the kids about west African dances and the art of playing the talking drums of Nigeria.

Her personal life might be in shambles, but seeing the kids' excited faces was the bright spot in her day.

Chapter Twenty-Four

As soon as Skye entered the coffee shop, the heady scent of freshly ground coffee beans and baked goods like blueberry muffins and vanilla biscotti filled the air. The place was packed. Patrons sipped coffee while scrolling through their phones, working on computers, or huddled in groups of three or four engaged in intense conversations.

Her eyes landed on Monica seated at a table, scrolling through her phone.

The first time she called Skye and asked to meet, Skye hadn't wanted to see her because it was too painful. When she called again several days ago, Skye readily agreed. Not only because she missed Monica, but because she longed for information about Ethan and the woman she saw him with on TV. She shouldn't care, but curiosity gnawed at her insides and jealousy consumed her thoughts.

Monica cast a glance at the door, and as soon as she saw Skye, a smile broke out on her face. Skye waved, genuinely happy to see the younger woman, and signaled toward the register to indicate she was going to buy a cup of coffee.

She ordered an iced coffee and then wound her way through the tables to join Monica. They hugged briefly, and she sat down opposite her friend with her back to the large window that showed the passersby on the street.

"How have you been?" Monica asked, a huge grin on her face.

"Great," Skye said, hoping her answer was believable.

She hadn't gotten much sleep lately, her confidence taking a beating after seeing Ethan with that woman. She kept wondering if he'd taken her to the suite at The Rose Hotel or invited her to the house. Maybe they'd had breakfast in the sitting room off the bedroom—an area she'd decorated to be comfortable and welcoming—as much for her as for Ethan. She couldn't stand the thought of that woman sitting in the chairs that *she* picked out.

"Are you really great?" Monica's left eyebrow lifted into a perfect arch. "You look... like you've lost weight."

She'd lost a few pounds but didn't think the weight loss was that noticeable. "I've um... been so busy lately, sometimes I forget to eat." She let out a clearly manufactured laugh, but it was the best she could do.

"Are you sure you're okay?" Monica's eyes filled with worry.

"Of course. I'm fine. I'm *wonderful*. Couldn't be better." Skye forced a brighter smile onto her lips. "Enough about me. What's going on with you?"

Monica told her about her latest sponsorship deal on Instagram and informed her about Sunday dinner. "Thiago surprised us and came home. He's staying for a while to complete consulting work for a major client." She fell silent for a moment. "I didn't invite you for coffee to talk about my family. I miss you." The expression in Monica's eyes was raw and honest.

"Oh, sweetie, I miss you too."

"Just because you and Ethan are done, doesn't mean we have to be done."

Skye chose the next words carefully. "I'd like to stay in touch, but it's best if I keep some distance, particularly since it's obvious Ethan has moved on already."

Monica sighed despondently. "You're talking about the mystery woman he took to the foundation event?"

Skye could only nod, as her stomach tightened into a painful ball.

"I didn't see the news. Mommy told me about it. As far as I know, they're not serious."

Skye waited a beat, plucking off pieces of a napkin and then asked, "Who is she?"

"Her name is Vanessa. That's all I know. She hasn't been to the house or anything. None of us know her," Monica said placatingly, probably sensing Skye's distress.

"It doesn't matter. It's none of my business." It was a mistake to ask about the woman. She didn't want to hear anymore.

"Are you and Ethan done, done?"

"We are," Skye said firmly.

"Why?"

She almost didn't want to answer. "Honestly, because I want to get married, and he doesn't."

"You do?" Monica's surprise proved to Skye that she had done a very good job of convincing everyone she didn't care about marriage.

She nodded.

"Why do you want to marry Ethan? He's so awful."

They both laughed.

Silence fell over the table.

Monica spoke first. "I feel terrible that I didn't know. I keep thinking about everything I said at Maxwell's graduation party. Me and my big mouth."

Skye waved a hand dismissively. "You're fine. To be honest, I used to feel the way you do, but over the years my feelings changed, and I have to admit that I want a ring. I want a more permanent relationship with Ethan. Except, *he* doesn't feel the same way."

Monica hummed her understanding. "I don't think he ever will either. Joanne really did a number on him."

The mention of his ex-wife's name jolted Skye. Her hands cradled the coffee while curiosity burned the tip of her tongue.

"What did she do? For the longest time the most he said was that she's the worst thing that ever happened to him, and he hoped to never see her again. While we were in Belize, he told me more. He thinks she used to cause allergic reactions by poisoning him with shellfish."

Monica's mouth fell open. "What?"

Skye nodded. "You didn't know?"

"Hell no, I didn't know. I swear, if I ever see that bitch..." She clamped her mouth shut and shook her head.

"If you didn't know about the shellfish poisoning, what did you mean when you said she 'really did a number on him'?"

"I don't think I'm the right person to tell you if he didn't," Monica said carefully.

"I won't repeat a word you say." Skye leaned closer, needing to know more. Needing the information she had been denied for so long. "I promise."

She hated to pressure Monica, but she had to know what else happened between Ethan and his ex-wife. What did she do to turn him into the man he became—a man who strongly rejected any notion of marriage?

Looking hesitant, Monica sipped her coffee to buy time. Skye didn't say a word, not wanting to inadvertently change Monica's mind if she edged toward divulging the information.

Finally, Monica leaned forward and whispered, "If you tell him I told you, I'll call you a liar and deny this conversation ever took place."

"I won't say a word, I promise," Skye said hurriedly. Then she crossed her heart to further confirm the statement.

Monica continued to whisper, as if anyone were paying attention to them. "You know they were married for three years, right?"

"He told me. He said they met in college."

"That's right, and they got married within months of graduating. Joanne was just really pushing for it. By then Ethan had already accumulated a pretty impressive real estate portfolio, but he wanted to wait on marriage until he was better established. Mommy didn't like her from the beginning, and Papa Ben tried to talk him out of marrying her."

"Why?"

"They believed they were rushing. I was still in high school and thought it was romantic they met in college and were getting married soon after. I did overhear my mother tell Papa Ben she thought Joanne was a gold digger. Ethan didn't listen to anyone. He gave in to Joanne's pressure and got married—to make her happy, I guess. Big mistake. She ended up cheating on him, with a competitor."

Skye's mouth fell open. "*What?*"

What woman in her right mind would cheat on Ethan? He was ridiculously generous, virile, sexy, had a commanding presence. She couldn't believe it. Joanne was way worse than she ever imagined.

Monica continued talking in a hushed voice. "The guy was older and worth more than Ethan. Way more because he'd been in real estate development longer—a family legacy kind of thing. Anyway, Joanne didn't just cheat on my brother. She gave her boyfriend sensitive information about a deal Ethan had been working on for months. He ended up losing the deal, and *he was livid.*"

Skye could only imagine. That might explain why he was always so careful around her when it came to his business. He allowed her into all aspects of his personal life but limited information he shared about his business interests, divulging only surface level details.

"Wow."

Monica shook her head in disgust. "Their break up was pretty bad. Ethan wasn't able to prove Joanne was having an affair, so he was forced to give her a big settlement when the marriage ended."

"On top of losing the deal and having her cheat on him? Ouch. Talk about rubbing salt in the wound."

"I know. I seriously worried about him during that period," Monica murmured. She gazed out the window over Skye's shoulder.

"You thought he might hurt himself?" She couldn't imagine Ethan committing such a drastic act, but one never knew the mental strain someone suffered under when deeply hurt.

"Oh no. I was worried he was going to put a hit out on her."

Skye snorted, and they both enjoyed a brief moment of giggling.

"That sounds more like Ethan," she said.

"As messy and awful as the divorce was, there was a silver lining. Ethan worked his butt off after that. To be honest, I believe she's the reason he's as successful as he is today, though I'd never say that. He might kill me. I believe he needed to show her that she had made a mistake, and he needed to come back from the defeat of losing a major deal."

"What happened to Joanne and the other man?"

"They got married about three months after her divorce from Ethan." Monica sucked iced cappuccino through her straw. "Less than three years after that, Ethan executed a hostile takeover of the guy's company and kicked him out. It was all over the financial news and was a bit more tabloid themed because his ex-wife was married to the man whose company he took over. All their old dirt came up. It was a mess, but Ethan came out on top. I have no idea where Joanne and her husband are now or if they're still married. Knowing her, she probably sank her claws into another unsuspecting fool. No way she stayed with that guy after Ethan took his business. One thing for sure, they both learned a valuable lesson. You do not cross my brother."

Skye took another sip of her drink and digested the information Monica had shared.

"Skye, I'm certain Ethan loves you. He's just scared—I'm sure he would never use that word—of getting hurt again."

Skye gave the younger woman a grateful smile. "I believe he loves me too, in his own way, but I can't imagine Ethan being scared of anything. If he is afraid of being hurt, that doesn't change how I feel. I want a husband and a family of my own."

"I understand. I guess one day you'll start dating some other man, but I hope we can still be friends. I mean, I know I give Ethan a hard time, but he's my brother and I love him and I think you're good for him. Definitely better than Joanne." She shivered. "I hate you're no longer together, *but* I understand you have to do what's best for you. Just know that I do miss you. I considered you part of our family. We all did."

An ache of longing burned in the middle of Skye's chest. "That's very sweet of you to say. I considered you my family too," she said thickly. She reached across the table and squeezed Monica's hand. "Ethan and I might be finished, but you and I will definitely remain friends, for as long as you like."

She was rewarded with a bright smile.

Later, seated in her car in the parking lot, Skye replayed the conversation in her head.

Just like Amy, Monica mentioned the possibility of her dating again. Maybe she *should* move on. What was she waiting for? Despite all his talk about getting back together, Ethan had moved on. So should she.

She blinked back tears. "What were you thinking? Did you really think he'd be sitting around, pining for you?"

Before they met, Ethan had earned quite a reputation with women—a reputation she learned about after the fact. She'd never had reason to doubt his fidelity, but now that they were no longer together, there was no reason for him to sleep alone. Not a man who enjoyed making love as much as he did, his appetite so insatiable, some nights she asked for a break.

Maybe she *should* call Trey. He was friendly, interested, and unlike Ethan, open to marrying again. He might be the next love of her life. If not him, someone else. At the very least, she could dip a toe in the dating pool and eventually swim into deeper waters once she became accustomed to life without Ethan.

Skye dialed the number of The Greasy Spoon and a man answered the phone.

"Hello, may I speak to Trey Patterson please?"

"He's not in. He went to pick up supplies. Would you like his cell number?"

"Oh, I don't know. I could leave a message—"

"He don't care. Got a pen?"

"I do. One minute." Skye fished a pen and paper out of her purse. "Ready."

The man gave her Trey's number, and she repeated it aloud before hanging up.

She hesitated for a few minutes, debating if she was being too pushy by calling Trey on his cell phone—a number he had *not* given her.

"I'm gonna do it."

She dialed his number, but the call went to voice mail. She didn't speak for a few seconds and almost hung up, but at the last minute she plowed through.

"Hi, Trey! This is... this is Skye Thorpe, from the Decatur Student Learning Center. When I was in The Greasy Spoon a while back, you sort of ask me out, and I, uh..." She laughed shakily. "I don't know why I'm so nervous. I guess I'm a bit out of practice, but I'm single now and wanted to see if your offer to get coffee still stands. If so, call me, and let's make plans."

She paused as she tried to think of something witty to say. Instead, she ended with her number and added, "I hope to hear from you."

Then she hung up.

Chapter Twenty-Five

Trey and Skye walked between the pillars leading to the entrance of Amy and Brian's home. After she left a message on his voice mail, Trey returned the call and they went for coffee one day. His sense of humor kept her laughing the entire hour and a half they spent together.

Tonight they arrived a little late because Trey's car wouldn't start, and he asked her to pick him up. If she hadn't been spoiled by Ethan, she probably wouldn't have minded, but Trey's request mildly surprised her. Ethan would have ordered a car and met her at Amy's house or picked her up in said ordered car. From the beginning of their relationship, he behaved like a gentleman and a leader. Some men took charge and solved problems, and that's the kind of man Ethan was. She was used to him handling issues so she didn't have to.

Immediately, Skye felt guilty for her uncharitable thoughts comparing the two men. Their unique personalities meant they handled situations differently, and she shouldn't compare Trey —a man she barely knew—to a man she'd been in an intimate relationship with for years.

164

"I can't believe this is their house. When we pulled up, I thought it was a hotel," Trey murmured.

If he thought Amy and Brian's home was large, he didn't want to see Ethan's bigger, grander estate.

"He's a successful real estate attorney," she told Trey.

He smoothed a hand down his white shirt. "Thanks for inviting me. I guess tonight I get to see how the other half lives."

The housekeeper opened the door and took Skye's red and black shawl, which she'd brought in case the temperature dropped later in the evening. The portly woman escorted them into the sitting room where the party was in full swing. Upbeat music poured through the speakers, and two couples danced like no one was watching.

Amy came over as soon as they entered and gave Skye a relieved hug. "I'm so glad you're here. I was worried you weren't coming." She looked lovely in a black and white cocktail dress, her long blonde hair practically shimmering under the lights.

"Of course I was coming. We had a little car trouble. This is Trey Patterson." Skye placed a hand on his arm. "Trey, this is Amy Nielsen, our somewhat frazzled hostess."

"Please don't tease me tonight. I feel like I'm still suffering from baby brain. It's so nice to meet you, Trey. I have to run, but when things calm down, I'll be back to chat. You guys help yourselves to a drink at the bar, and I'm going to rush into the kitchen to find out where the rest of the food is because the platters are almost empty."

Skye shook her head as she watched her friend rush off.

"She's not nervous at all," Trey said.

Skye laughed. "She's a sweetheart but a bit neurotic. Let's get that drink."

There weren't many people in attendance—approximately twenty—so they didn't have to wait long. The bartender fixed a white wine spritzer for Skye and handed Trey a frosted mug of beer.

They joined a conversation where two men argued about which country produced the most coffee in the world. One of them said Colombia, the other insisted the answer was Brazil. Trey agreed that Brazil produced the most coffee.

"What does the lady say?" one of the men asked, looking at Skye through his glasses.

She threw her hand up. "I honestly have no idea, but if I had to guess, I'd agree with Trey and say Brazil."

"How about we place a wager? Five bucks?"

"Make it ten and you have a deal," Trey said.

"Mr. Moneybags over here," Glasses said, jabbing his thumb in Trey's direction.

The other man, a redhead, pulled out his phone and searched for the answer. With a big grin, he said, "Brazil. You owe us ten bucks each."

"Oh come on!" Glasses snatched the phone and looked at the screen. "Damn, Colombia is third. Vietnam produces more coffee than Colombia?"

Trey held out his hand. "Pay up."

Glasses reluctantly dug out his wallet, while Skye hid her laughter behind her glass. Poor guy, she felt sorry for him but was leaving the party ten dollars richer.

As Glasses asked, "Anybody got change for a hundred?" Ethan appeared like an apparition in the doorway, and Skye froze.

The laughter died on her lips, and the activity in the room devolved into slow motion. Amy, standing across the room, looked genuinely surprised when she saw him. Her eyes found Skye's, and she mouthed the words, *I'm sorry.* Then she turned to her husband and thumped him on the shoulder.

"Oh, shit," Skye whispered.

"What's wrong?" Trey asked.

"My... ex just came in." She followed his progress in the room, throat dry and knees almost giving way. She wanted to run to Ethan and hug him and kiss him and slap him and knee him in the groin all at once.

Trey followed her line of sight to Ethan. "Is his being here a problem?"

"Not really. I wasn't expecting him, that's all."

"Here you go." Glasses handed her the ten dollars, causing a temporary distraction, but not for long.

Her eyes returned to Ethan, as if drawn by a magnetic force field. He looked stunning in all black—a black long-sleeved shirt and black trousers. She unnecessarily smoothed the hair at her temple, though there were no flyaways thanks to the soft gel she used to pull her hair into a bun.

Ethan glanced in her direction. Unsure of how to react, she let a faint smile touch her lips, but Ethan didn't smile back. His attention shifted to Trey, his gaze intense and lasting way too long.

After that, she pretended he wasn't in the room—a room that suddenly seemed too small for a man of his stature. More guests arrived, and over the course of the next thirty or so minutes, he made his rounds, shaking hands and greeting other invitees. Meanwhile, she and Trey moved on from the two men. She tried her best to concentrate on the conversation with Trey and the older woman to her right, but she fixated on Ethan's progress around the room.

The way he moved with quiet confidence and laughed as he charmed the other guests with his banter constantly drew her attention. Every time she thought he was on his way over to their little circle, the hairs on her arms puckered with goose pimples, and her heart fluttered like the wings of a dragonfly.

Finally, he strolled over to them, and the fist of nerves in her stomach expanded into the size of a beach ball.

"Ethan! How are you?" the woman beside her said.

"Estelle." Ethan shook her hand.

Skye had never met her before tonight's event, but she wasn't surprised Ethan knew the woman. He knew everyone and remembered the most minute details about people he encountered.

"Don't tell me you came alone. Where's Richard?"

Estelle shook her head regretfully. "Feeling under the weather, unfortunately. I'll be sure to tell him you asked about him."

"Please do. We'll have to get out on the golf course again soon. It's been too long."

"He'll love that. If you will excuse me, I need to refresh my glass."

As soon as the older woman left, Ethan's gaze landed on her. "Hello, Skye."

"Hello, Ethan." Her voice came out huskier than expected.

Tension crackled between them.

Trey shoved his hand into the middle of the circle. "I know you and Skye have history, so let's cut through the awkwardness now. I'm Trey Patterson. Nice to meet you."

Skye was impressed by his forthrightness, but Ethan stared at his hand for a smidge too long, and for one horrifying moment, she thought he'd leave Trey hanging. Then a semblance of a smile crossed his lips, and she breathed a silent sigh of relief.

He shook Trey's hand. "Ethan Connor. Connor International Industries. I'm in real estate development, and you?"

"Nothing quite so sexy. I own a restaurant called The Greasy Spoon."

"The Greasy Spoon... That name is familiar," Ethan said slowly.

Skye almost rolled her eyes at his acting.

"Is that the one you and Thresa go to for lunch from time to time?" he asked Skye.

"Yes," she answered. As if he didn't know.

"So you've heard about me," Trey said.

Ethan studied him, eyes keen with interest. "Not you, but certainly your restaurant. After seven years, there's not much Skye and I don't know about each other."

"Seven years. That's a long time." Trey looked at her with surprise, as if this new information concerned him.

"Sometimes people grow apart," she said, to put his mind at ease. "We didn't work out."

"So she says," Ethan drawled.

His response startled Trey, whose gaze jumped between them, obviously searching for clarity because he sensed an undercurrent.

Skye's eyes shot daggers at Ethan. "Trey, could you excuse us? I need to speak to Ethan in private for a few minutes."

"Oh... uh, sure. I'll get another drink from the bar." Frowning, Trey slipped away.

Skye swung toward Ethan. "I—"

"How long have you been seeing him?" he interrupted.

"None of your business."

"Actually, your relationship with him is my business, because he came here with my woman."

"We're not together. You and I are broken up."

"Correction, we're on a break, which you requested. Maybe I should have established parameters such as not screwing anyone else."

"I'm not—" Skye took a deep breath. "I can date whomever I want."

"You're not supposed to be dating anyone," he said in a menacing tone.

"Are you the only one allowed to date, then?"

His brow furrowed in confusion.

"Don't play dumb, Ethan. I saw you with your new girlfriend, the one you took to the Johnson Foundation event. She was showing a little too much skin, don't you think?" She sounded catty. Disgusted with herself, Skye drained her glass.

"I see the claws have come out," he drawled. "You saw the news, I take it. For your information, Vanessa—that's her name—and I are not dating. She's one of the contractors I do business with. We happened to be going into the venue at the same time and walked in together."

"She was hanging all over you," Skye said, hating herself for her accusatory tone and the obvious jealousy in her voice.

"I offered her my arm because the tile floor was slippery, and she was wearing a new pair of shoes."

He had an explanation for everything.

"That's all?"

"Yes, that's all. No reason for you to be jealous."

"I'm not jealous!" she snapped. "I don't care about her or any woman you choose to see."

"You're a terrible liar."

Okay, so she had a jealous, possessive streak where Ethan was concerned. She was no fool. She saw how women looked at him, and he enjoyed the fruits of his labor—bespoke suits, Ferragamo shoes, and Patek Philippe watches. He was always well-groomed, hair neatly trimmed, and smelled so good at times she simply wanted to press her nose to his skin and inhale.

"I'm jealous too. When Brian alerted me that you were coming and bringing a date, I wasn't happy. I certainly didn't expect to see you wearing my favorite color on you while standing next to your date." His voice dropped lower as he undressed her with his eyes. "You look incredible. The color and sleeveless design reminds me of the Oscar de la Renta gown you left hanging in your closet." His eyes ate her up from head to toe.

A frisson of heat passed over her skin. That look reminded her of the softness of high-thread-count sheets at her back and Ethan's powerful body thrusting into hers.

"Stop looking at me like that. I'm here with someone else."

"Mr. Greasy Spoon?" he asked derisively.

"His name is Trey."

"Whatever his name is, he must be out of his mind for leaving you alone with me. That's a sign of weakness. You deserve better than that."

"I know exactly what I deserve, and I intend to get it. Do me a favor."

"Anything," Ethan said, eyes lowering to her breasts.

The unfettered hunger in his gaze threw Skye off kilter, and she inhaled a choppy breath. "Stay the hell away from me tonight."

She walked away, leaving him alone and going to stand beside Trey.

Chapter Twenty-Six

Being in the same place as Ethan was harder than Skye expected. She was wound so tight a ball of tension settled between her shoulders.

She needed air. She needed time away from his orbit.

Excusing herself, she slipped away from the music and guests, going down a quiet hallway toward a restroom in the back of the house. She stepped inside and was about to lock the door when it was pushed in from the outside.

She stepped back in surprise to see Ethan standing before her and watched in consternation as he flipped the lock. They occupied the outer part of the restroom, in a sitting area that contained a couple of chairs. A counter with two mirrors were at her back, a convenience for anyone who simply wanted to pop in, check their makeup, and pop out without using the bathroom.

Ethan took a seat in one of the chairs and crossed his right ankle over his left knee as if they were about to have a chat about a mundane topic.

"I came back here to be alone. Would you please leave," Skye said.

A slow, knowing smile filtered across his lips. "You don't want to be alone. You knew I'd follow, and you wanted me to follow you."

"Someone has a very high opinion of himself."

"Someone knows his woman very well."

"I'm not your woman anymore."

"You'll always be my woman. You've been mine since we met at the bar in my hotel."

His eyes roamed over the red cocktail dress. It was sleeveless, with a fitted bodice and waist and a hemline that fell below her knee in a full-skirt design. She didn't waste her breath again telling him to stop ogling her because he wouldn't care. He did as he wanted, when he wanted.

"I have a question about Mr. Greasy Spoon."

"His name is Trey."

He looked steadily at her and spoke deliberately, tension vibrating in every word. "I asked you about him after the play at the learning center. You said he was just an acquaintance, but I remember you talking about that restaurant, how the food was unhealthy but so good. The fries are delicious, the burgers are juicy. Did you have a crush on him?"

"No."

"Did he have a crush on you?"

"I... He might have. I don't know." Skye shrugged.

"You're lying, Skye. You know I hate lying."

She leaned against the counter, defiantly refusing to respond.

"Were you sleeping with him when you and I were together?" Ethan asked in a suspiciously soft voice.

"What difference does it make now? You and I are done," she taunted.

His jaw tightened, and a storm brewed in the dark depths of his eyes. "I asked you a question. Were you fucking him while we were together?" The profanity was a surprise as anger slipped into his voice.

Too late, Skye realized she'd simply been waving a red flag in front of a raging bull. Her conversation with his sister came back in a flash, and she immediately regretted the recklessness of her response. Ethan was sensitive about cheating because his wife had cheated on him.

"No."

He shot to his feet, and she took a startled step back.

"Don't lie to me. Were you *fucking* him while we were together!"

"No!" she yelled back.

She had never seen Ethan so emotional. The Ethan she knew rarely lost his cool, and even when angry he became colder, downright emotionless. He also rarely cursed. She cursed way more than he did and could count on one hand how many times she'd heard him utter anything as colorful as the word fuck. For him to drop the f-bomb twice meant he had been pushed beyond his limits. She wanted to scream that she wasn't Joanne but wasn't supposed to know those details about his past life.

"I never cheated on you. I swear."

The fire in his eyes dimmed, and Ethan crowded her against the counter. She stood very still.

"Are you sleeping with him now?"

"No."

He tilted up her chin with his right hand, eyes boring into hers.

"*No*," she repeated.

"You better not be lying to me, or I will break every bone in his arms. We'll see how well he flips burgers then." The fingers of his left hand flexed, as if ready to break Trey's arm now.

"You're not a violent person."

He tilted his head, gaze swallowing her whole. "I'm not, but I would commit unspeakable acts of violence for you."

His words chilled her, but a small primitive part of her brain thrilled at the threat of such characteristic behavior.

Ethan released her and put distance between them. Skye breathed easier as tension trickled from her body.

He shoved a hand in his pocket and rested his butt against the counter. "It's time for you to move your things back in. I should have never allowed you to leave." He smoothed a hand down the front of his shirt.

"You didn't allow me to leave. I left of my own accord. I *chose* to go."

"And I let you."

His words infuriated her.

"You always have to have the last word, don't you?"

He watched her from the corner of his eye. "Should I prove it to you?"

"How could you—"

He stepped toward her, and her back pressed against the wall.

"Should I?" Ethan came closer, bringing them within inches of each other. "The other day you came by my office, angry about the apartment situation, yet you and I both know I could have spread you on my desk and had you as many times and as many ways as I wanted, until you were sobbing my name."

"You arrogant asshole."

His head lowered to hers, and his breath kissed her lips. "Should I prove it to you?" he whispered.

175

She couldn't move, could hardly breathe—mesmerized by his words and the intensity in his eyes.

He twisted her toward the mirror so she could see the reflection of the two of them in the glass.

"What are you doing?" her voice trembled.

"Do you want me to beg?" Ethan kissed her bare arm, the entire time watching the two of them.

Skye remained still, unmoving, anxious to prove that he no longer held power over her.

Beneath her dress, his hand slipped up her outer thigh, fingers gliding higher to cup her throbbing sex in a blatant display of ownership. His touch was possessive, dominating, demanding her capitulation to his will.

She gasped. "Ethan..."

He fastened his teeth into her neck, like a lion taking steps to secure its prey.

When he licked the gentle bruising, she shivered, and her heart galloped as excitement overtook the logic of her brain and she succumbed to the sensual power he wielded.

"Push me away if you want me to stop," he said softly. "But you won't, because you need this as much as I do. Look at how hard you've made me." He pushed his hardening length into her ass, and an involuntary whimper escaped her throat.

His left hand covered her breast and her mouth fell open, her head falling back to his shoulder. He pinched her nipple between his fingers and made her whole body ache as the sensitive flesh puckered into a tight peak against the fabric of her dress.

Skye felt trapped in a maze of both pleasure and pain. Lifting onto her toes, she rubbed her bottom against his erection. Right then, the doorknob rattled, and she bit down on her bottom lip to keep from crying out. The fear of getting caught heightened the excitement.

She wanted him, needed him. There was no high like being with Ethan. Being with him created an adrenaline rush greater than sky diving or riding a motorcycle one hundred miles an hour down a crowded street.

As he slowly stroked her swollen sex, she practically dripped, panting with need and the desire to come.

"Look at yourself in the mirror and see all the beautiful faces you make as you enjoy yourself. You see how it is with us? It's nothing to run from. It's nothing to be ashamed of."

A swipe of his size thirteen shoe forced her legs wider.

Thighs trembling, Skye plastered her fingers on the counter and lifted her hips into the rough caress of his hands.

"Bend over, sweetheart."

His husky command was a prelude to sin.

Skye dropped onto her forearms, and he lifted her dress high on her hips. He palmed her bare ass and groaned low in his throat as she arched her back in a blatant plea for him to touch her. His moist lips sucking on her left ass cheek made her sex clench, and when he licked the crack of her ass, she let out a loud moan and trembled.

"You belong to me, Skye," he whispered against the base of her spine. "And I don't beg for what's mine."

Her forehead touched the cool counter, and she closed her eyes. The sounds of Ethan undoing his pants made her knees wobble, and she waited in agony for him to take her, bent over the counter with her legs spread and him behind her.

He was in too much of a hurry to remove her thong. He simply dragged the damp material aside and inserted his body into hers. They both moaned at first contact.

He slid in with ease, her entrance damp and widening to accommodate his thick length. He was velvet-covered steel and felt so good. Her bottom pressed flush against his hips. In the mirror she watched the way his nostrils flared and the naked play of emotions on his face as he concentrated on giving them both unbelievable pleasure.

Ethan started slow, but as they became more aroused in the race to climax, he fucked her harder and faster, his blunt fingers biting into the softness of her hips—dragging her back as he thrust forward with jackhammer-like precision. A wail of pleasure broke from her throat, and her hands pressed down onto the counter.

Ethan bent over her, his lips at her ear. Their eyes locked in the mirror. "See? It's not over between us," he panted.

Skye came hard, quakes of ecstasy erupting through her as she spasmed around his huge dick. Another cry of passion broke from her throat, breath stuttering as she shuddered through the unrelenting climax. It was almost too fast, but she'd been starved of him for twenty-nine long days.

Ethan came right after, burying his face in her neck and releasing a husky groan as his hands tightened on her hips.

He fell onto one forearm behind her, his breathing as labored as hers.

They stayed in that position until their heart rates returned to normal.

Chapter Twenty-Seven

After they cleaned up, Skye stood in the middle of the room, arms folded over her chest. So much for standing her ground and staying strong. Her so-called resolve had been laughably weak, easily buckling under the weight of Ethan's magnetism and her own desire for his touch.

Ethan dried his hands and tossed the paper towel into the trash. "Tomorrow is day thirty. You might as well come home now. I can make arrangements to have your things brought back to the house," he said matter-of-factly.

Skye turned away, disgusted with herself. She should have forced Ethan to acknowledge her value. Instead, she recognized her own weakness for him. Less than thirty days and she folded like a sheet of paper.

"I miss you. Is that what you want me to say?" He whispered the words. "Being without you is driving me out of my mind. This has been the longest month of my life." He kissed her bare arm, and his soft lips made her skin tingle. "Tell me you don't miss me. Tell me you don't want to come home, where you belong. Tell me what just happened between us means nothing. You say those words, and mean them, and I'll walk out of here and never bother you again."

He would do it too. Ethan never said anything he didn't mean, and the thought of him walking out of her life for good terrified her. Knowing she would never speak to him again, never again experience the out-of-control passion they'd shared moments ago suddenly became the worst torture imaginable.

His face remained impassive. Devoid of emotion as he awaited her answer.

"You didn't wear the watch to the fundraiser. You always wear the watch with your lighter colored suits."

His features softened in a way uniquely reserved for her. He never looked at anyone else like that.

"I took it to the jeweler for repair. It's back in my possession, and the next time I wear a tan, cream, or brown suit, I will place it on my wrist like always."

It was a small thing, but his answer meant the world to her. He hadn't cut her out. He hadn't erased her from his life. The watch had been out for repair.

Gazing up at him, Skye kept her arms crossed over her chest, protecting herself from the fallout of the answer to her next question. "Did you sleep with her—Vanessa?" she asked in a small voice.

"No. I haven't touched another woman since we met. Why would I, when I have you?"

His answer brought tears to her eyes. What woman could resist such a beautiful sentiment, particularly from a man who could have anything he wanted?

He cupped her jaw with one hand, and his eyes filled with soft affection. He kissed her tenderly, his mouth moving gently over hers. He gave the best kisses. His lips grazed her jaw and then the side of her neck.

"I can't wait to get you home, back in our bed so we can make love properly." He placed another soft kiss to her cheek and then took her hand.

Her gaze landed on their entwined fingers. The past month had been difficult. She'd missed Ethan and the life they shared. But gazing down at her ringless left hand, a hollowness filled her chest. Her hand would remain like that indefinitely. Though she longed to return to him, nothing had changed.

"I'm not coming back," Skye said softly.

He gave a little laugh. "Of course you are," he said arrogantly, confidently. "If you're worried about your friend out there, I'll handle him."

She couldn't look at him. "Ethan, let me go."

Silence filled the room. She stood there with her head hung low, needing him to do the right thing. To set her free.

She tried to slip her hand from his, but his fingers tightened.

His breathing became labored. "Skye, what are you saying?"

She sniffed and blinked away tears. "I just want you to let me go."

"Look at me!"

She lifted her head and met his gaze. She couldn't quite decipher the emotion she saw. Fury, panic—a little bit of both.

"After what we just shared? Obviously there's still something between us. It's been twenty-nine days already—I'm miserable, and I know you are too. Why put us both through anymore torture?"

If someone had asked her what the worst feeling in the world was, she could honestly say it was looking into the eyes of the man you loved and feeling your heart splinter.

"Let me go, Ethan." Her lower lip trembled. "Please."

His eyes widened fractionally, and he stepped back as if

someone shoved him. He swallowed hard, eyes never leaving hers. "I *can't*," he said in a strangled tone, as if the same someone had wrapped their fingers around his throat.

"You have to, because I'm not strong enough to walk away —obviously." She laughed briefly, a mirthless sound of resignation. "It's time for us to move on from each other."

"So you can find someone else?" he demanded with a flare of temper.

"Yes," she replied, though she doubted she'd find anyone as appealing and charismatic as Ethan, who consumed her the way he did. "You need to find someone who fits your lifestyle and makes you happy."

"*You* make me happy," he said.

"I need to find someone who can give me what I want. We spent seven years together, and that's longer than most relationships, and longer than many marriages."

"I love you."

"I know, in your own way."

"Not in my own way," he grated. "You make it sound as if my feelings aren't real."

"Your love isn't enough for me. I'm no longer satisfied in our relationship. I'm no longer happy, so you *have* to let me go, because you can't give me what I need." Tears burned the inside of her throat and nose.

He stared at her in disbelief, the quiet stretching between them.

"I'm sorry, Ethan, I can't. I just can't anymore."

His square jaw tightened. His gaze dropped to the floor, and his shoulders slumped in a sign of defeat.

Skye stepped over to him and captured his head in her hands and pressed her lips to his.

One last kiss. He didn't kiss her back. His mouth remained hard and unyielding.

"Goodbye, Ethan," she whispered.

Then she walked out.

* * *

When Skye returned to the party, Trey asked where she had disappeared to, and she apologized, mumbling something about needing to take a break.

She expected to see Ethan again, but after thirty minutes he didn't make an appearance, and she realized he'd left.

At about eleven, the party started winding down as the couples said goodbye. As often happens, other couples expressed their regrets and left, each one citing their own unique reason—kids at home, a long day, plans in the morning, and other unnecessary explanations which meant they were simply ready to end the night.

Trey and Skye became one of those couples. Skye retrieved her shawl, threw it across her shoulders, and hugged Amy goodbye.

"Had a great time," she said.

"Thank you for coming, and I'm so sorry about... you know," Amy said, worry in her eyes.

"Don't worry about it. You didn't know he was coming, and it's not the end of the world. His appearance didn't spoil my evening at all."

"Good to hear. Take care, and we have to do lunch one day soon."

"Definitely."

On the thirty-minute drive to Trey's apartment, they made small talk. Trey recapped his conversations with other guests and expressed how much he enjoyed the evening. Skye responded where appropriate, the entire time wondering how to let him down easy.

When they pulled up in front of his apartment building, Trey turned to face her. "Would you like to come up for a drink?"

"It's late, and I should go home."

"I understand. I really enjoyed myself tonight, Skye, and I'm looking forward to spending more time with you. I feel like this is the start of something good between us."

Skye racked her brain for a polite way to let him know there wouldn't be a next time, and they weren't about to *start* anything. She wasn't ready for another relationship yet. She needed time to heal from the break up with Ethan.

Trey leaned in for a kiss, and she dodged his mouth.

He made a sound of surprise.

"I'm sorry," Skye said. "I thought I was ready, but I'm not."

He slumped in the seat. "The ex?"

She nodded. "Letting go is harder than I thought."

"I understand. I didn't stand a chance against that guy, anyway."

She averted her eyes rather than admit he was correct.

"I guess I'll have to settle for you coming into the restaurant and having lunch. Goodnight, Skye." Trey squeezed her hand and then stepped out of the car.

Skye watched him walk away, taking comfort in the fact that she'd made two good decisions tonight.

Chapter Twenty-Eight

Phone to her ear, Skye rolled over in the bed, eyes swollen from crying all night. She'd done the right thing, but that didn't make the decision any easier.

"What did you say?" she asked to the Midtown Towers manager on the line. She couldn't have possibly heard what she thought she heard.

"I said, we had an opening on the waiting list and the one-bedroom apartment you requested is now available. Are you still interested?"

Skye sat up in bed and pushed her hair out of her face. "Yes, I am. But I don't understand, when we spoke before, you gave me the impression there was no chance an apartment would become available any time soon."

"If I gave you that impression, I'm sorry. We didn't have anything available at the time, and I didn't want to get your hopes up. Because of an unexpected vacancy when one of our tenants moved out, a premium apartment is available. It includes a fireplace, a den, and free concierge services."

"I thought the concierge services were an add-on."

"Typically, yes, but those fees have been waived for you. You can submit your application online, and then we'll need a small deposit to hold the apartment."

Stunned, Skye didn't know what to say. The other day she was hunting for an apartment and getting shut down, today she could have an apartment in her first-choice complex.

"Miss Thorpe?"

"Yes." Skye shook her head to dispel the cobwebs. "I'm... interested, and I'll work on the application today."

"Excellent. If you have any questions, call the main number and dial my extension—7745. Midtown Towers looks forward to having you as one of our residents. Enjoy the rest of your day."

Skye set the phone on the bed. She should be ecstatic, but instead, her shoulders slumped and her heart hurt.

Ethan must have intervened. He was leaving her alone. Giving her what she asked for so she could move on.

Then why did she feel as if someone had put a hole in her chest?

Skye's bottom lip trembled, and she buried her face in the pillows for another bout of sobbing.

* * *

Ethan found his mother in the garden cutting okra off her plant and dropping them in a green basket at her feet. She wore loose-fitting jeans, a long-sleeved plaid shirt, and wide-brimmed hat.

"You can take the girl out of the farm, but you can't take the farm out of the girl," he said, crossing to where she stood, careful to step over her pumpkin vines.

Rose glanced at him over her shoulder. "That's right. Look at these beauties, they're my best batch yet." She cut off another one and dropped it on the others. Scooting the basket along the ground with her foot, she said, "I didn't know you were coming by."

"I hadn't planned on it, but I was out and thought I'd swing by and say hello."

"Well, I'm glad you did." *Snip. Snip.* "That's probably enough for today. Your Aunt Florence is coming by later for these. Let's go up to the house."

Ethan carried the basket until they reached the two steps leading to the terrace. He placed the basket on the tile, and he and his mother sat on the top step.

Rose placed her hat beside her and smoothed the edges of her rumpled hair. "So, what's the real reason you're here?"

"What makes you think I'm here for any other reason besides spending time with you?"

"Because I know my son. What's wrong?"

Ethan expelled a deep breath. "Skye left me... for good."

Rose placed a comforting hand on his arm. "Oh honey, I'm sorry. What happened?"

"She wants to get married, and I..." He blew out another breath. "You know how I feel about marriage."

"Yes, I do." Rose took in the view before them, the garden sectioned off in a huge, multi-acre back yard bordered by trees. "Your first marriage was a disaster."

"Complete hell. I was married to a caricature of a villain. Lucifer himself."

"The devil incarnate."

"Beelzebub."

"Satan."

They both laughed, and she hooked her arm through his.

Ethan rubbed the back of his neck. "I should have listened to you and Benicio."

"You should have, but you were young, only twenty-two years old and thought you were in love and didn't think your parents knew what they were talking about. I knew who Joanne was, and I know Skye is nothing like her. Skye loves you. She loves you so much she spent seven years in a relationship without any guarantees. That's not easy for a woman, in a society that tells us marriage is the ultimate goal and the way to achieve real happiness. If Skye were like Monica, living together without a formal commitment wouldn't be a problem. However, Skye is not like your sister. She *wants* to be married, probably more than the average person because she lost her parents so young. You have to let go of the bitterness of the past and recognize Skye is an upgrade."

"I know she is." He spent most of the past day thinking, after he left the party Friday night.

"Then why don't you treat her like one if she wants to be your wife and you love her? Do you love her enough to give her what she needs? Not what you want to give her, but what she's asking you for. You often refer to her as 'my Skye.' She needs you to be 'her Ethan,' to know that you're hers. She needs a ring."

Ethan examined his left hand. That finger had been empty for a long time.

"Can you imagine spending the next thirty years without her by your side?" Rose asked gently.

Ethan let out a little laugh. "I've barely managed to survive the thirty days we spent apart."

Rose patted his forearm. "I believe that's your answer."

Ethan knew what he needed to do. He'd known all along, but the bitterness of the past had held him in a chokehold. His own anger and negative experience had dictated his behavior toward Skye, which wasn't fair to her.

They remained quiet for a while, his mother keeping an arm wrapped around his, her way of letting him know she remained present and ready to talk more if needed.

"What's going on with you and Benicio?" Ethan asked.

Rose shot him a sideways glance. "Nothing."

"Nothing, huh?"

"That ship has sailed. Your stepfather and I are in a good place, and it's best not to rock the boat."

"You don't have to be alone if you take Benicio back."

She paused, a frown between her eyes. "Are you suggesting we should remarry?"

"You and he belong together, Mom. You love each other and there's no reason why you should be apart—like you pointed out with me and Skye. Do you think you could give him another chance?"

"Of course we love each other, but sometimes love isn't enough."

The sadness in her eyes and the heaviness of her words cut through him.

"It should be," he said.

"It should," she agreed. "We were supposed to grow old together, but your stepfather is a difficult man, and he has his ways and I have mine. I thought about taking him back, but then decided we're good the way we are. We get along much better now. I'm not constantly sniping at him about not spending enough time with me or holding in my comments because I don't want another fight."

"But you're not happy."

"I am happy, because I'm doing what's best for me. Ben is doing what's best for him. Sometimes people grow apart." She shrugged. "That's just the way it is."

"But you said you still love him," Ethan reminded her.

Rose laughed, shaking her head as if recalling a private joke. "I'll always love that man, but our relationship has evolved, and we're better off as friends. Sometimes it's better to walk away because being together makes you too miserable. That's not the case with you and Skye, though. I can tell."

"You think you'll remarry?"

Rose fell silent for a moment. Finally, she lifted her gaze to him. "To be honest, I haven't thought about it. Marrying again... it's not something I think I want to do at my age."

"You're never too old..."

"Maybe, but this old bird does not see another marriage in her future," Rose said, amusement in her voice. "No more talk about me. What's the plan for Skye?"

"I need her in my life, and it's time for me to let go of the past."

"Are you saying what I think you're saying?"

"Yes, and you're the first to know. I'm going to ask Skye to marry me."

His mother's eyes lit up, and she let out a squeal of happiness. "Oh my goodness, Ethan! You know how much I love Skye, and I would love for her to become part of the family. It's not easy to recognize mistakes and change from them. I'm proud of you. You and Skye belong together, and now that you realize that, there is nothing that should keep you apart."

"If she hadn't left me in the first place, I wouldn't have realized what I was missing."

"Sometimes, that's what it takes. Sometimes you have to lose what's most important to you to appreciate it. That's how I know Ben and I are done. If Ben wants to come back home, he knows what to do, but he hasn't done it. Which says to me that he has made his decision about what is most important, and what is most important is not me. But *you've* figured out what's most important, and you know that it's Skye. I would love to officially have her become a part of our family. I have no reservations about you marrying her."

"Now all I have to do is convince her to take me back," Ethan said.

Chapter Twenty Nine

Thunderous applause followed Ethan to the front of the room. He waved his hands to indicate the audience should pipe down, and the clapping stopped. He scanned the faces looking back at him. Levar Bettari, one of his investor-partners, organized the event in his hotel ballroom. Ethan suggested a smaller gathering but agreed to Levar's request, which resulted in over two hundred people in attendance.

Phase one of Horizon was complete, and tonight this group of men and women were going to celebrate that accomplishment with him. Levar provided plenty of food—mushroom bites, shrimp poppers, vegetable trays, and a plethora of other choices, not to mention a fully stocked bar and champagne for the toast.

Daria was in attendance, and so was his personal assistant, Layla, an attractive woman with tawny-beige skin and long dark hair. He knew well there were people who speculated about their relationship, but they'd never crossed the line.

Managers and supervisors from the construction site were

included on the guest list and everyone looked forward to the food and promise of a party to take place after the speeches ended. Ethan planned to disappear long before the debauchery began.

The only thing missing was Skye. Normally, Ethan wouldn't have brought her to this business-related event, but she would have celebrated with him later. Perhaps at a nice restaurant or at home after she and Mona prepared a congratulatory meal.

She had no idea he'd reached the major milestone he'd worked toward for years. Knowing he wouldn't hear her soft voice—*I'm proud of you, baby*—crushed his spirits, a painful reminder of all he lost by letting her walk out of his life.

"If you've known me for any length of time, you know I'm not one for long speeches, but I think we can all agree it's a great relief to have wrapped up the first phase of this project. Many of you know how important Horizon is to me. It's my largest development to date, and an economic boon for this part of the city. We had the opportunity to create something different, innovative, and we accomplished that. Together. I could not have done this project without all the separate pieces working in harmony, and there are so many people who helped make this possible but are not here tonight.

"From the construction workers, to the engineers, to the messengers, the janitors—to all of you—including my right hand, Daria, my executive assistant, and my left hand, Layla, my personal assistant. Every single one of you helped hold this thing together. I won't talk too much longer, except to let you know how grateful I am for all your hard work, and I'm looking forward to the next couple of years, when we complete phase two and three and end up with a community we can all be proud of. So to each and every one of you I say, thank you." Ethan raised his glass of champagne. "To the next chapter."

"To the next chapter," most of the group chorused, while others whooped and hollered.

Levar reclaimed his place at the front of the room, a short nerdy-looking man with spiky black hair. "Thank you, Ethan. I, for one, am looking forward to the next couple of years. Now, ladies and gentlemen, let the partying begin!"

Cheers went up in the room, the lights dimmed, and the music started.

Daria walked over and peered up at Ethan. "Nice speech. Short and sweet. I'm sure everyone appreciates your brevity, because now the partying can commence." Her critical eye roamed the group. Already, ties and jackets had been removed, causing their owners to loosen up as they gyrated in the open space commandeered as a dance floor.

"It's about to get wild up in here," Layla said.

"That's my cue to leave. I'll see you next week, Ethan. Good to see you, Layla."

"Good to see you too."

Daria waved as she left.

"Have you eaten?" Layla asked. She, Daria, and Skye were always concerned about him eating because he skipped meals when he became too busy.

"Not since lunch."

"I'll fix you a plate. Mushrooms and vegetables sound good? There are meatballs and boneless wings too," she said.

"Just mushrooms and a couple pieces of chicken."

As she walked away, Ethan removed his phone from his pocket and checked the screen. He didn't know why he bothered. Skye wouldn't call. He thought about calling and giving her the good news but changed his mind and returned the phone to his pocket. That conversation could wait. He had a plan regarding their reconciliation, and he didn't want to veer too far from it.

Layla came back and handed him a small plate of food and a fork.

"Thank you. You should go. I'm only going to stay for another ten minutes or so."

"I don't mind sticking around. You never know, you might need me to do something."

"I can't imagine there's anything left to be done tonight." Ethan ate several of the mushrooms.

She went by the house earlier and brought him the clothes he wore—a black jacket and clean white shirt, no tie.

"Well, if you're sure..."

"I'm positive."

"All right. You have a good night."

The music became ridiculously loud, and Ethan made up his mind to leave. He ate a piece of chicken and searched the dim interior for Levar, catching sight of him holding a bottle of beer while engaged in a conversation with the construction foreman. Ethan made his way over to them, absentmindedly scratching the side of his face.

"I didn't want to leave without saying good—" The inside of his wrist itched.

He tugged back the sleeve on his jacket and saw inflamed skin, raised bumps all over.

The plate of food dropped to the floor, and chicken and mushrooms scattered across the carpet.

"Ethan, what the hell?" Levar stared at him.

The itching became worse, and pretty soon his eyes would swell and his lips would distort into a cartoonish size.

"Layla. Do you know where she is?" He whirled around in a panic, heart racing out of control in a frantic search for his assistant. Like Skye, Layla always carried an EpiPen in her purse. If she was still here, he could counteract this attack.

"I think she left. I saw her go out—"

Ethan rushed toward the exit.

"Ethan!" Levar called.

Ethan stumbled out the door. Where the hell was Layla? He shouldn't have sent her home.

"Ethan!" Someone called his name again from a distance. Levar? Or was it someone else? He couldn't tell as a dizzy spell hit.

He stretched out a hand to the wall to keep from falling and pulled out his phone. His driver answered on the first ring. "Halston, I need you in here. Main ballroom. Now."

"On my way."

Levar grabbed his arm. "Ethan, what the hell is going on?"

"Hospital," Ethan croaked, loosening the shirt's top button.

The world was spinning, and he couldn't keep up with the rapid rotation. Back against the wall, he breathed heavily as his airway started to close. He tried to pull oxygen into his body, but his lungs refused to cooperate.

Halston appeared.

"Hospital," Ethan repeated.

The driver nodded. "I've got you, Mr. Connor." Halston grabbed him under the arm and hustled Ethan out the door.

Curled up on the sofa in her hotel room watching TV, Skye ignored her ringing phone. Too lazy to lift her head from the pillow, much less go all the way across the room to get her purse, she snuggled deeper under the soft throw as she binge-watched a crime series.

A lease agreement sat on the table before her, unsigned. She'd made no move to move out of the hotel since her conversation with Ethan, despite the call from Midtown Towers to let her know about the 'unexpected vacancy.'

She felt unable to act or make a decision. Numb, but not numb enough to avoid the painful squeeze her heart made every time she thought about Ethan.

A tear slid from the corner of her eye and over the bridge of her nose, and she roughly wiped it away. No more tears. Somehow she always survived the day, but at night, memories tormented her and kept her from rest. Maybe she should go back to him.

No! she thought immediately. She needed to give herself time to get over him. She only really walked away for good a week ago.

The call went to voicemail and almost immediately started ringing again. Someone really wanted to talk to her. She considered ignoring it but then wondered if something could have happened to one of her cousins in California.

Tossing off the throw, Skye scrambled to her feet and picked up her purse. Holding the phone aloft, she frowned at the unfamiliar number.

"Hello?"

"Hello, may I speak to Skye Thorpe?"

"This is she."

"Hello, Miss Thorpe, I'm Nurse Niles at Emory Decatur. Ethan Connor was admitted to the hospital thirty minutes ago—"

"What?" Alarm grabbed her heart, and she clutched the back of the armchair next to her. "Is he all right? What happened?"

"He's fine now," the woman said, keeping a soothing tone to her voice. "He had a severe allergic reaction to something he ate and lost consciousness at the hospital—"

"He lost consciousness!" Skye exclaimed.

"—but he's perfectly fine right now. He regained consciousness and is resting. His driver is here, but you're listed as his emergency contact, so that's why I'm calling."

"I-I'm on my way." Skye spun in a circle, temporarily disoriented before rushing over to the closet to search for shoes.

The nurse gave Ethan's room number and Skye repeated it before hanging up and shoving her feet in a pair of tennis shoes. She'd never known Ethan to lose consciousness before. This must be really bad. She grabbed her purse and keys and fled out the door.

She made record time driving to the hospital, hoping and praying a cop didn't pull her over. When the elevator opened on Ethan's floor, she rushed down the sterile white hallway, bypassing the waiting area and went straight to the desk.

"Hello, I'm Skye Thorpe." She showed her I.D. "I received a call that Ethan Connor was admitted less than an hour ago." She gave the room number. "Can I see him?"

"I'm Nurse Niles. I spoke to you on the phone. Mr. Connor is sleeping. The antihistamines we gave him make him drowsy. We'll need to keep him overnight, but you can go in and see him." She told Skye how to get to the room.

"Thank you."

Before Skye could walk away, a male voice called her name. She turned to see Halston standing before her.

"Halston, oh my goodness. How did this happen?"

The big man shrugged. "Mr. Connor was at the Bettari Hotel celebrating the completion of phase one of the Horizon development."

"Layla always has an EpiPen. Was she not there?"

"He sent her home early."

"Of all the nights..." Skye shook her head. "Thank goodness you were there. Have you called any of his family?"

"No, ma'am. I was waiting until you arrived. Would you like me to do that?"

Skye took a moment to breathe and calm down. Ethan was fine. If only her heart would stop racing. "Actually, call Layla, let her know what happened, tell her I'm here. I'll get in touch with Ethan's family and update them once I have a chance to check on him. In the meantime, you go. You've done enough for the night."

"Are you sure, ma'am? I can wait."

"No, go. I'll stay with Ethan. Thank you." She touched his arm in gratitude.

"Not a problem. If you need me, please call."

"I will."

After he left, Skye followed the nurse's directions to Ethan's room. She entered quietly and gazed down at him. There was swelling around his eyes and lips, as if he'd gone several rounds with the heavyweight boxing champion of the world. Otherwise, he seemed to be resting comfortably.

Her heart constricted painfully at the thought that she could have lost him. She longed to gather him in her arms and bury her face in his neck, but went to sit in the chair by the window. If Ethan was staying the night, so was she.

Then she dialed his mother's number.

Chapter Thirty

E than woke up extremely groggy and slowly, the room came into focus. He was in a hospital. A TV hung on the wall across from him. The last thing he remembered was eating at the Horizon event and breaking out in hives. After that, everything else was a blur.

He caught movement at the corner of his eye.

Skye.

She sat in a chair near the window, texting.

His heart took off like a racehorse. What was she doing here?

"How are you feeling, Mr. Connor?"

The voice came from his left. A pleasant-sounding nurse stood beside the bed. She checked his pulse rate by holding his wrist in one hand while she looked at her watch.

"Alive."

She laughed. "Very good. The swelling in your face is almost gone. You went into severe anaphylactic shock, and we used a combination of antihistamines and steroids to relieve your symptoms and take down the swelling. The IV in your arm provides fluids to increase your blood pressure, which dropped drastically and caused you to pass out right as you arrived at the hospital. Lucky for you, you have a very skilled driver who got you here in record time. You were only out for a minute or so."

They had effectively brought him back from the brink of death, though she didn't use those words. That was the worst attack he'd had in years. He rubbed his face, fighting the urge to scratch because his face and arms still itched.

Skye remained silent the entire time.

The nurse continued. "We need you to stay overnight for observation, to make sure the symptoms don't return."

"I understand. I've been here before and know the drill."

"Good. Then you know once you're released, no strenuous activity for at least twenty-four hours. I'll be back to check on you in a couple of hours. If you need anything before then, press the button and either I or one of the other nurses on staff will come right away." Another pleasant smile before she walked out of the room.

Ethan studied Skye, who dropped her gaze to her phone. He had a hard time reading her emotions.

"Hey," he said.

Skye lifted her head. "Hi."

She spoke in a husky voice, like someone who had been screaming for hours, and she seemed tentative, scared.

"This is a surprise."

"You never removed me as your emergency contact, so they called when you were admitted."

"Oh." Ethan resettled to a more comfortable position against the pillows. "Is Halston still here?"

"I sent him home, and um... I let your family know you were admitted." Her voice wobbled, and she looked on the verge of tears.

"I'm okay, Skye."

She'd never known him to have such a bad allergic reaction before. During the course of their relationship, he'd only had a couple of minor incidents where he felt an allergic reaction coming on and used the epinephrine auto-injector right away to relieve the systems. He acted so fast the incidents resulted in only minor swelling around his eyes, which disappeared within hours.

"I feel like I jinxed you." Tears filled her eyes.

"Sweetheart, you didn't."

"I made that stupid joke in Belize, and then you said your ex-wife—"

"Come here."

At the gentle command, she rushed to his side and came down onto the bed beside him.

"I've never been so terrified in my life," she sobbed into his neck. Her tears dampened his neck.

He curled an arm around her waist and drew her soft body closer. He brushed his nose against her forehead and drew in the sweet scent of her skin. "I'm fine. I'm okay."

Skye lifted her red-rimmed eyes to his. "Not to be dramatic, but you could have died."

"I'm too stubborn to die."

Skye roughly rubbed away the tears from her cheeks. "How could this have happened? You've been fine in every hotel you've visited over the years but have an allergic reaction at your own event?"

"I ate a few mushrooms and a piece of chicken, but there was shrimp on the menu. There must have been cross contamination with the shrimp and one of those things."

"Whoever prepared the food should be fired," Skye said angrily. "You could have died."

"I know all the stats about my condition. Only one or two

percent of people who experience anaphylaxis die. It's not that common, though it can cause serious complications. An attack can happen anywhere at any time. This was a fluke."

"I don't care about your percentages. That so-called fluke could have killed you."

He wiped away a tear from her cheek with his thumb. "But I'm not dead. I'm alive."

Ethan brushed his thumb across her cheekbone. Her reaction to his attack was so different from what he'd experienced with Joanne.

He remembered all the times he had an allergic reaction when he was married to his ex-wife. Her expression of indifference as she jabbed the EpiPen in his thigh was branded into his brain. It had taken a long time for him to admit the truth, but she had hated him. Maybe not in the beginning of the marriage, but certainly by the end.

He gently rubbed Skye's back to calm her. "I'm glad you're here."

"I'm staying the night," she said.

"Are you sure?"

Skye lifted her head, a fierce, warrior-like expression taking over her face. "Of course I'm sure. If they tell me I have to leave, they'll have to drag me out, kicking and screaming."

Ethan smiled at her, and she smiled back.

"I'm not going anywhere, Ethan," she said softly. "Get some sleep." She rested her head on his shoulder, and her body relaxed into his.

Ethan closed his eyes. The oppressive weight of loneliness and loss suffocating him finally lifted, and he breathed easier.

For the moment, at least, he had his Skye back.

203

The hospital discharged Ethan before noon the following day, and when Halston arrived to pick him up, Skye also climbed into the back of the limousine. Her presence in the car was as natural as if she'd never left and provided much needed comfort.

Neither said a word about her returning to the house. No heavy conversations about their split and where they should go from there.

Ethan instructed Halston to stop at Skye's hotel, where she packed a bag to take to the house. At the mansion, Mona greeted them at the door.

"How are you feeling Mr. Connor?" she asked.

"A little tired."

Skye threaded her fingers through his. "The doctor said he should get some rest, no strenuous activity. He's had a severe shock to his system, so he's going to take it easy the whole weekend." She looked pointedly at Ethan when she said the last part of the sentence.

Mona nodded. "Understood."

"Do I get a say?" Ethan asked in an amused voice.

"No, you do not," Skye said. "Mona, something light for lunch. Maybe sandwiches and soup or salad."

"And for you, ma'am?"

"I'll have the same. Could you have our meal sent up in about an hour?"

"No problem."

Ethan climbed the stairs with Skye, oddly pleased to have her take charge for a change.

In the bedroom, she said, "While you're in the shower, I'll let your family know you're home. Anything else you need me to take care of?" She hoisted her leather duffel bag onto the bed.

Ethan

He didn't answer at first, watching the back of her head as she rummaged through the contents in search of some item.

"No, I have everything I need."

He went into the bathroom and took a refreshing shower. When he returned to the room, Skye was nowhere to be found, but she had laid out his blue pajamas on the bed. He put them on and climbed under the sheets, hoping she would soon join him. The doctor warned about strenuous activity, which he knew included sex, but he longed to hold Skye in his arms. They had spent too much time apart.

Ethan closed his eyes, thinking he'd rest for a bit, but eventually fell asleep.

Chapter Thirty One

On Saturday, Ethan searched the news for any mention of his collapse but found nothing. Because his allergic attack took place outside the ballroom and away from guests' eyes, the persons knowledgeable about his trip to the hospital were Halston and Levar, and Layla had called Levar, asking him to maintain Ethan's privacy and not share what happened. The only news he found about the party specified the reason for the celebration and the high-profile names in attendance—Ethan, Levar, and a few others. Ethan didn't do much the whole day, but Rose and Benicio came by before nightfall and stayed for dinner.

Sunday morning before dawn, Ethan woke up to Skye nibbling on his ear, half on top of him, a hand inside his pajamas, stroking his junk. He groaned and smoothed his palm under the satin nightie she wore and squeezed her bottom.

She had spent the past two days with him, rarely leaving his side, but they hadn't made love in all that time. He was fully recovered, but Skye worried about his 'condition.' If the way she touched him and writhed against him was any indication, those concerns were out the window.

"You're awake?" she whispered huskily.

"Oh yes."

Together they worked his pants lower, and he held his breath while Skye's full lips wreaked havoc from the center of his chest down to his pelvis. Ripples of pleasure quivered under his skin as her tongue played with his belly button and she brushed her lips along his length. Her actions were nothing short of torturous, and the urge to shove between her lips became an almost unbearable burden.

Finally, she used her hand to guide him into her wet mouth, and he gripped the sheets in a valiant fight to stave off an untimely ejaculation. She swallowed his whole length in a constant refrain of back and forth, plunging from the tip to the base in a heady combination of sucking and licking.

Ethan whispered words of encouragement past his tight throat, letting her know how good her mouth felt and praising the way she performed on his dick. Hand at the back of her head, he surged upward, groaning as he fucked her mouth. Their gazes meshed and tangled in the almost black room, and more ripples of pleasure made their way under his skin.

Skye sucked him eagerly, humming in the back of her throat and cupping his balls to encourage his release.

"Sweetheart." The one word spoken in a pained, raspy voice signaled he neared the end of his tether.

She pulled harder, and the chains of restraint snapped.

Ethan exploded, his warm cum spilling into her mouth. He came so hard and fast he temporarily lost his senses and his fingers tightened in her hair. The entire time he shuddered through the climax, her mouth remained glued to his shaft to brazenly drain him of every bit of his strength.

Limp and flat on his back, Ethan breathed heavily and

fought to regroup. Meanwhile Skye crawled back up the bed and rested her soft body atop his. The self-satisfied smile on her face indicated she knew her own power and reveled in the ability to bring him so quickly to orgasm.

"Witch," he muttered, and slapped her on the ass.

Burying her face in his neck, her soft laughter whispered over his skin. Ethan squeezed her bottom and kissed her temple.

"Your turn," he said in a low voice.

He brushed aside a swath of hair so he could kiss the side of her neck, and she made a soft sound of pleasure.

After she wiggled out of her nightie and panties, Ethan rolled Skye onto her back. He preferred making love to her with the lights on so he could see every inch of her tawny-gold flesh, but he accepted the circumstances for the moment, anxious for a chance to possess her luscious body.

He kissed the tops of her breasts while one hand squeezed her bottom. She was soft and smelled like a rose garden, and his need for her burned with the heat of a thousand suns. He sucked on her brown nipples and let his hands freely roam the curves of her voluptuous body.

Working his way lower, Ethan kissed the rounded slope of her belly before sucking on her lower abdomen, right above his goal. Her moaning and feminine scent made him harder than the white marble in the bathroom. Dragging his tongue into her wetness, he committed a tender assault.

Skye let out a soft mewl, arching her breasts toward the ceiling as she lay open so he could feast on her tender flesh. Gently, he kissed and pleasured her with his mouth but had no intention of allowing her to come that way. Oral sex was simply a shortcut to foreplay because he wanted inside of her so bad.

He made his way back up and dipped his tongue into her mouth. "See how good you taste," he said huskily.

She clasped his face in her hands and sucked on his tongue, panting and groaning as they engaged in a sloppy wet kiss. She wrapped her legs around his hips, and the tip of his erection touched her entrance. Ethan sank his hard length into the sweet prison between her legs. When her muscles flexed around him, he shuddered and she cried out. Fire licked at his spine at the audible sound of her pleasure.

Ethan slid deeper, her muscles stretching around his engorged flesh and a louder cry of pleasure exploding from her lips as she arched toward the ceiling.

Rocking inside her, he rubbed her swollen clit with his thumb, using her body's own juices as a lubricant to push her over the edge.

She came almost instantly, crying out with abandon, her hips jerking with rapid-fire speed as she rode the peaks of ultimate pleasure. Ethan came soon after, his body erupting into hers in a shuddering climax that had him burying his face into the scented hollow of her neck.

Later, he held her close, kissing her nose and cheeks. She hummed her pleasure.

"Baby," she whispered.

His arms tightened around her, and he wondered how in the world he had survived without her for so long.

* * *

Curled around Skye's back, Ethan rubbed the length of her arm to her wrist. He couldn't seem to stop touching her.

"I've been thinking, and I've decided to give up shellfish," Skye said.

"There's no need for you to do that," Ethan said.

"I want to."

"You're going to give up lobster ravioli at Notte?" he asked, voice filled with skepticism.

"Yes," she said vehemently.

"It's your favorite dish. Every time you eat it, you rave about the creaminess of the sauce and the chunks of lobster in each bite. You don't have to give up what you enjoy, sweetheart. I've gone seven years without a major incident. I had a good run. I'm sure I can go another seven without an episode. I don't want you giving up the things you enjoy for me."

Skye remained silent, plucking at the white sheet.

"At least I can tell Mona to be extra vigilant."

"Mona knows, believe me."

"I want to do something," Skye whispered.

"You already have." He kissed her shoulder. "You've been by my side the whole time."

They fell silent.

"You did much more for me than my ex-wife ever would have."

She went still, and though it was tough, he forced himself to open up. This conversation was overdue.

"Joanne and I married young, only a few months after we graduated from college. I did everything I could to make her happy, not realizing at the time that what made Joanne happy was having more material possessions. She saw the wealth of my family and the money I accrued myself and wanted in. But I was just a stepping stone for her. She was after bigger fish and found that fish in a competitor. I won't go into the sordid details, but she ended up having an affair with this man and shared information with him—sensitive information I confided in her about my business—which allowed him to cut me out of an important deal. Our marriage lasted three years, and I was forced to give her a big settlement to get rid of her."

"I'm sorry that happened to you," she said quietly.

"It was a tough lesson to learn."

"What happened to them?"

"They got married a few months after she and I divorced. Less than three years after she left me, I took over his company and kicked him out."

"Do you know where they are now?"

"They divorced not long afterward. I don't know where he is, and I don't care. A few years ago, I did learn, against my will, that Joanne remarried and lives with her new, older husband in Sweden."

Skye twisted around to face him in the dark. "I don't know how people like her sleep at night."

"I'm pretty sure she doesn't. Satan doesn't need to sleep."

She snorted, humor filling her eyes in the dark. "You really hate her."

"Hate might be too mild of a word."

She laughed again and slowly sobered. "I was thinking... I should move back in," she said in a small voice, as if there was some chance he might reject the offer.

"Is that really what you want?"

She nodded, playing with a hair on his chest. "This is where I want to be. With you."

"This is where I want you to be. I never wanted you to leave."

"I know." She smiled in his eyes.

He kissed her soft lips. Then her chin and the top of her throat. She curled a leg across his hip, and he slowly caressed the length of her thigh—knee to pelvis—taking pleasure in the smooth softness of her skin. Rolling her onto her back, his kisses continued along the arch of her throat and across the crests of her full breasts. Damn, his woman was sexy.

"Again?" she breathed, voice sounding simultaneously amused but strained with hunger.

Ethan licked her right nipple while filling his palm with her left breast. He squeezed and sucked at his leisure, listening to her soft moans as she writhed beneath him. "I need to make up for lost time," he whispered over one delectably aroused peak.

He buried his face in the scented valley of her pillow-soft bosom while sliding a hand between her legs to cup her wet sex. He inserted the two middle fingers, slowly priming her for his entry. Minutes later the fingers were replaced with his hard length, and eventually, the only sound in the darkened room were her short, sharp cries as he brought them both to a shattering climax.

Chapter Thirty-Two

F irst thing the next morning, Ethan took breakfast on the balcony in blue pajamas, two heating lamps boxing him in to counterbalance the chill in the air.

His mother insisted he keep them up to date on his progress, so he sent a group text to the family letting them know he was taking the day off but going back to work on Tuesday. Monica complained his text woke her up too early, but ended the message with *I love you* and half a dozen heart emojis. Texting didn't satisfy his mother, so he spent fifteen minutes talking to her on the phone, during which she expressed her pleasure that he and Skye were back together.

As he sipped coffee and turned his attention to the financial news, Skye exited the French doors.

"Good morning," she chirped.

Because she didn't have all her clothes at the house yet, she wore his robe. She was a thick woman, but the robe was still oversized on her, and while the hem landed around his knees, it fell almost to her ankles. She looked adorable.

"Good morning," he returned. "Since I'm off today, we should get your things from the hotel."

"After breakfast?" she suggested.

"That sounds good. Did you sleep well?"

"Mhmm." Skye stretched her arms above her head.

"The usual for breakfast?"

She nodded and picked up a strip of bacon he hadn't eaten. "Instead of strawberry jam, I'm in the mood for apple butter this morning."

Ethan opened the internal communication app on the iPad and sent Skye's breakfast request to Mona.

Skye rested her elbows on top of the concrete balustrade, gazing out over the back of the property. "Did you have Layla call the tree company like the landscapers suggested?"

Ethan kept his gaze on the screen in front of him, scrolling through news headlines. "I forgot. I'll have her do it tomorrow."

"Baby, I told you about that weeks ago. If that tree is rotten and falls, it'll crash into the carriage house. I'll take care of it."

He glanced up. "You sure?"

"Positive."

He placed the tablet on the table, following her movements as she poured orange juice in a glass and settled in the chair across from him. They'd fallen back into their normal routine so easily. As if the time apart never took place.

"What?" she said, juice halfway to her mouth.

"It's good to have you home."

"It's good to be home." Her eyes softened as she looked at him.

"I'll be right back," Ethan said.

He went into the bedroom and didn't take long before returning to his seat.

"Come here, Skye." He patted his right thigh.

A playful pout on her lips, Skye walked over and sat on his

lap. Draping her arms around his neck, she asked, "What did you have in mind?"

Ethan took a moment to think before he spoke the words on his heart.

"I missed you, and I'm glad you came back to me, but I don't want you to have doubts about my feelings for you or our future together." He reached in his pocket and removed the velvet box he retrieved when he went inside.

Her eyes widened. "Ethan...?"

He flipped open the box and exposed the sparkler inside. He'd chosen a rare, emerald cut light-yellow diamond. Seventy round, brilliant cut white diamonds ran around the rectangular shaped rock and down the upper shanks of the platinum band.

Skye gasped, covering her open mouth with both hands.

"Will you marry me?"

She burst into tears and wrapped her arms around him, sobbing into his neck. Ethan held her tight in his arms until she stopped crying.

Finally, she sniffled and nodded against his chest. "Yes," she whispered.

He slipped the ring on her finger, and she held out her hand, admiring the way the jewelry sparkled in the morning light. She turned to him with watery eyes. "I love it. I love you."

Arms around his neck, she kissed him thoroughly and tenderly.

Shortly thereafter, Mona appeared on the balcony, carrying Skye's breakfast on a tray. As she set the food on the table, Skye showed off the ring. "Look, Mona. We're getting married, and you're the first to know."

Mona's face broke into a smile. "Congratulations to you both. It's good to have you back, Miss Thorpe."

"Thank you. It's good to be back," Skye said.

Mona disappeared, leaving them alone.

"I'm surprised she didn't tell you how hard it's been to cook for one person," Ethan muttered.

"Why would she say that?" Skye asked.

"That's what she said to me multiple times since you've been gone. Her passive aggressive way of telling me she wanted you back, as if she didn't cook for one before you moved in."

His declaration tickled Skye, and she had a good laugh.

After breakfast, they spent the rest of the morning calling and talking to family members, letting them know the good news. After the phone calls, they went to the hotel and picked up Skye's clothes. They made a second stop to the storage facility for her other personal effects. Ethan checked in with Daria and Layla to plan the rest of the week while Skye and household staff members unpacked her belongings and put them all back where they belonged.

They spent the rest of the day reading in the sitting room and then watched a couple of movies in the theater room. Ethan was utterly content. His woman, his fiancée, his wife-to-be was home, and his life was finally back to normal.

So when he rolled over in the middle of the night and didn't make contact with Skye's soft, warm body, he frowned and stretched a hand across the bed. All he encountered were the cool sheets. He was alone.

His eyes flew open, and he sat up in a panic.

Where was Skye?

He hopped out of bed and pulled on his boxer briefs, heart beating a rapid tattoo in his throat. He was on his way to check the contents of the dressing room when he noticed one of the French doors ajar. He peered out and saw Skye standing at the end of the balcony bundled in a jacket and his pajama bottoms. Her forearms rested on the cement balustrade, eyes fixed on the darkness of the trees surrounding the property.

Ethan slipped on a robe and walked into the cool fall air to join her. She faced him and smiled, but in the near darkness he recognized the smile didn't reach her eyes.

"What's wrong?" he asked.

A sad little smile lifted the corners of her mouth. "Are you sure, Ethan? Are you sure you want to do this?"

No need for an explanation. He knew exactly what she was referring to and hated that doubt persisted, though he'd confirmed his love and given her the promise of his heart forever.

"I'm sure."

"Obviously, this is what I wanted all along, but now that I have it..." Her eyes dipped to the yellow stone on her hand. "I don't want to pressure you into marriage. I want you to *want* to marry me."

"I admit, I didn't want to be coerced into marriage. I'm a bit... stubborn."

"No kidding," she said.

He gave her a pointed stare, and she clamped her mouth shut.

"You were right all along. I let the bitterness from my first marriage color *our* relationship and keep a wall between us. You're nothing like my ex, and I should have asked you to marry me a long time ago. I not only hurt you, I hurt myself by keeping walls in place. When I didn't have you in my life anymore, it shocked me into understanding how much you mean to me. Then you came back to me, even though I didn't give you what you wanted. That's not a sacrifice I want you to make, and marrying you is no hardship. Marrying you will be the best decision I've ever made."

Tears shimmered in her eyes. "Better than investing in Horizon?"

"One hundred times better." He came closer and took both her hands in his. "I want to spend the rest of my life with you, bound together by that piece of paper I thought I didn't want. You're the woman I want—need—as my wife, and the woman I want to start a family with. Don't doubt that."

"I don't. Not anymore," Skye whispered.

"Good. Now will you come back to bed? Your fiancé doesn't like sleeping alone."

A smile broke out on her face. "Fiancé. I love the sound of that." Skye raised up on her toes and gave him a soft kiss.

Taking her hand, Ethan led her into the house and closed the door behind them.

Also by Delaney Diamond

Ethan Connor was first introduced in the story about his personal assistant, Layla Fleming. Read her happily ever after with Rashad Greene in What She Deserves, a second chance romance.

More family series are available!
Visit my Books page to learn about the
Johnson Family
Brooks Family
Hawthorne Family

Audiobook samples and free short stories available at
www.delaneydiamond.com.

About the Author

Delaney Diamond is the USA Today Bestselling Author of sensual, passionate romance novels. Originally from the U.S. Virgin Islands, she now lives in Atlanta, Georgia. She reads romance novels, mysteries, thrillers, and a fair amount of nonfiction. When she's not busy reading or writing, she's in the kitchen trying out new recipes, dining at one of her favorite restaurants, or traveling to an interesting locale.

Enjoy free reads on her website. Join her mailing list to get sneak peeks, notices of sale prices, and find out about new releases.

Join her mailing list
www.delaneydiamond.com

- facebook.com/DelaneyDiamond
- twitter.com/DelaneyDiamond
- bookbub.com/authors/delaney-diamond
- pinterest.com/delaneydiamond

Made in the USA
Monee, IL
12 March 2022

92795383R00125